PRAISE FOR *MICKEY*

"Chelsea Martin continues to prove herself the preeminent chronicler of Internet age malaise and I fucking love it. *Mickey* takes her provocative poetry long form, weaving the tangled tale of a breakup that shouldn't be as confusing as it is. This has replaced *Anne of Green Gables* as my cozy times reading. Who the fuck knows what that says about me, but it says a LOT about the power of Chelsea's writing."

—**Lena Dunham,** creator of HBO's *Girls*

"Chelsea Martin's *Mickey* is beyond superlatives but I'll use them anyway: intelligent, hysterical, elusive, an exquisite original. If you enjoy thinking, laughing, and self-loathing, read this book."

—**Chloe Caldwell,** author of *Women* and
I'll Tell You in Person

"There is no other writer who makes me laugh out loud more than Chelsea Martin. Both hysterical and heart-wrenching, *Mickey* is a well-rounded, hyper-realistic portrait of heartbreak in the age of the Internet."

—**Mira Gonzalez,** author of *I will never be beautiful enough*
to make us beautiful together

PRAISE FOR *EVEN THOUGH I DON'T MISS YOU*

"Martin's *Even Though I Don't Miss You* is also funny, and tragic in the way that staring at the Internet until you pass out in a pile of Doritos crumbs is tragic. Her deceptively relaxed prose perfectly captures the Facebook-guzzling void that constitutes modern heartbreak. Fav."

—Lena Dunham

"About halfway through, I said, "This book is giving me feelings."

—Mary Miller, author of *The Last Days of California*

"Martin's a brooding minimalist who is great on relationships, the choreography of neurosis, and the feedback loop between selfishness and self-abnegation."

—Justin Taylor, *Vice*

Mickey

A novella by
CHELSEA MARTIN

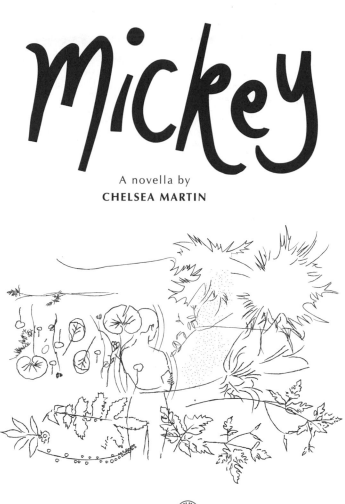

CURBSIDE SPLENDOR

CURBSIDE SPLENDOR PUBLISHING

Published by Curbside Splendor Publishing, Inc., Chicago, Illinois in 2016.

First Edition
Copyright © 2016 by Chelsea Martin
Library of Congress Control Number: 2015948138

ISBN 978-1-940430-73-7
Cover image by Danny Espinoza
Author photo by Kaliisa Conlon and William Schultz
Edited by Naomi Huffman and Catherine Eves
Book design by Alban Fischer

If You're Gone
Written by Rob Thomas
(c) 2000 EMI BLACKWOOD MUSIC INC. and BIDNIS, INC. (BMI)
All Rights Controlled and Administered by EMI BLACKWOOD MUSIC INC.
All Rights Reserved International Copyright Secured Used by Permission
Reprinted by Permission of Hal Leonard Corporation

Manufactured in the United States of America.

www.curbsidesplendor.com

MICKEY

"It's all gonna end and it might as well be my fault"
—"3AM," Matchbox 20

Things were already falling apart with Mickey anyway. I sensed it.

I invited Mickey to go to Jono's party with me. Once we arrived, Mickey and I argued about why we were there.

What is the name of that feeling when you feel the same feeling over and over and over and over until you don't even know what feeling the feeling is supposed to signify anymore?

"There isn't some specific reason why we are here," I told Mickey. "We are here because doing things like this is the kind of thing people like us do, and if we don't do things like this once in a while, then frankly, I don't know who we are."

"Who are we," I repeated, "if we are not the kind of people who go to this kind of thing when we're invited to it, if for no other reason than to be at a place like this under these kinds of circumstances?"

Mickey dropped it.

Jono approached me while I waited for the bathroom and told me he liked my boots in what sounded like a sarcastic tone. He scrunched up his face into a demonic smile. I complimented him on his level of drunkenness.

"Thanks," he said, looking into my eyes. "You, too."

Jono was waiting for me outside of the bathroom.

I touched my butt cheeks to make sure my skirt wasn't tucked into my tights.

"What kind of boots would you call those?"

"I don't know," I said. "Punk combat?"

"Are you a punk?"

"No."

"What are you?"

"Juggalo," I said. Jono laughed in a way that made me think he might not know I was joking.

"I'm joking," I said.

"I don't get it," he said.

"Never mind."

I put on my makeup and rested my face in my hands so the makeup would get slightly smudgy and uneven. I didn't want to look like I was trying to look good for my breakup.

I didn't want to seem like the type of person who got any pleasure from causing pain, or that I wanted to add to that pain with beauty—even my subtle brand of beauty.

I began to feel physically ill, which is often how my body responds when I have to do difficult things. I tried to appear as if I weren't feeling ill so that no attention would be paid to my physical comfort, so that Mickey could project onto me any feeling he wanted to make himself feel better or worse or vindicated (or whatever he wanted) as I broke up with him.

But I really did feel sick.

"I want to just be friends, I think," I said.

"Oh," he said. I resisted the urge to explain myself. We sat on my bed silently for a few moments.

"Is there something wrong?" he said.

"No, I'm in a weird place. I need some space, I think."

I folded my body as quietly and gently as possible to accommodate the pain in my stomach.

I value breaking up with someone because of the time it affords me to contemplate all the bad decisions I've made and exploit them for creative content.

I considered drawing a portrait of Mickey, just to find out how I would draw his face directly after our breakup.

What features would I spend a lot of time on, and which would I approximate? Would his expression turn out sad? Or would it look somewhat relieved, maybe indicating that he is eager to move forward with his life?

Then I considered making a portrait of Jono, though he grew less and less interesting to me every time I conjured his image in my mind.

I decided to make a portrait of Rob Thomas. I executed the portrait while looking at a staged, professionally lit photograph I found online.

I used a RoseArt crayon to draw some roses around his face.

Possible title ideas:

THIS PORTRAIT OF ROB THOMAS IS HOW I'VE CHOSEN TO DEAL WITH THE VERY REAL PAIN I'M FEELING.

I GUESS I'M JUST TRYING TO MAKE MYSELF FEEL BETTER TEMPORARILY INSTEAD OF DIRECTLY ADDRESSING MY PROBLEMS.

DRAWING WITH ROSEART CRAYONS IS ACTUALLY CON-SIDERED AVANT GARDE IN SOME CIRCLES.

PLEASE KEEP ME IN MIND WHEN GIVING OUT GENER-OUS ART GRANTS.

I showed Courtney my Rob Thomas drawing and she said it made her sad, which made me feel like she could see into my soul, in a bad way.

It made me want to do a better job covering up my soul and making elaborate excuses for the parts that could still be seen.

But if Rob Thomas' face can't cover up a sad soul then I'm all out of ideas.

I knew that Jono had a girlfriend because I had heard his friends say a girl's name before, sometimes followed by or preceded by the phrase "Jono's girlfriend."

Also because I stalked Jono's Internet profiles and saw a lot of photos of them together.

And also because I lurked the girlfriend's profiles and saw that she sometimes wrote posts that referred to a person named Jono in a romantic-seeming way. Sometimes she specifically used the word "boyfriend," and sometimes she tagged Jono in the posts, on which he would favorably comment—once, notably, with, "I love you."

I thought of her as I held Jono's hand on his couch one night. I think her name was Denise? I thought of how horrible and powerful I would seem in her eyes if she knew I was holding her boyfriend's hand.

She was, like me, pretty in a way you had to spend years learning to appreciate. Maybe that was Jono's type.

"Did you used to be fat?" I said.

"Yes," Jono said. "How did you know?"

"Oh, I didn't know. I just thought I'd ask."

"What do you mean?"

I laughed.

Jono tickled my ribs and we rolled around on his couch, still holding hands as he leaned over and pressed his face and black greasy bangs into my shoulder and breathed hot air onto my neck.

Then Jono's roommate came out from a back room and Jono was suddenly three feet away from me on the couch, staring absently into a phone that had materialized.

"What are you going to do tonight?" Jono said to his roommate.

"I'm not sure," the roommate said. "What are you going to do?"

"I have to go to my studio and finish a sculpture," Jono said. Then to me, "Do you need a ride home?"

"No," I said. "I can walk home."

I want to have an art show called I FIND MYSELF SO INTER-ESTING.

All the pieces will have titles like:

ISN'T THIS SUCH AN INTERESTING DETAIL ABOUT MY-SELF?

I THINK I'VE CAPTURED MY SARDONIC APPROACH TO MY OWN LIFE PRETTY ACCURATELY IN THIS ONE.

THIS ONE IS ABOUT MY TORTURED AND UNSUSTAIN-ABLE INNER LIFE.

ANOTHER REFERENCE TO MY CHILDHOOD!

HOPE THIS PIECE MAKES YOU SCARED TO TALK TO ME BE-CAUSE THAT'S MY FAVORITE INTERPERSONAL DYNAMIC.

I'M NOT BRAVE ENOUGH TO EXPOSE MYSELF IN A NON-ART SETTING.

HAHA! I JUST NEVER STOP BEING INTERESTING.

I don't even care if there's wine and cheese at the opening. I just want complete control of how I'm interpreted as an artist and human person, and to leave no room for anyone to project anything of their own onto me.

But I'd be really surprised and disappointed if there wasn't cheese at the opening.

In the movie version of my life there should be a group of confident-looking people standing in front of my work saying, "Seminal," to each other over and over.

And they should definitely include that word a few times in the trailer for that movie so people know what to expect.

And it would be good if they could cast someone unseemly to play the role of me, because then I would have someone tragic to compare myself to for the rest of my life.

The girl I presumed to be Jono's girlfriend posted to Jono's Facebook profile an hour after I had seen him, saying, "I miss you," and he commented back almost immediately, saying, "I miss you, too."

I called Mickey and got his voicemail and didn't leave a message.

You can tell when I'm going through something emotionally taxing because I will act very natural and unaffected.

I walked to the liquor store and bought three kinds of chips and two kinds of sparkling water.

I thought of the calories in the chips giving me the energy I would need to send Courtney text messages from the other side of the apartment.

I thought about the chips being digested and transformed into my skin flakes or fingernails or uterine lining. These chips were going to turn into me in symbolic and metaphysical ways.

When people are young they think nothing is going to hurt them, and nothing ever does, and gradually they realize that the hurt is coming from within.

And within, there are only chips.

I ran in to Jono in the grocery store and made some comment like, "That sure is a lot of peanut butter."

His apartment was close by, he said. We walked there and had sex in the bathroom.

"You don't have to leave," he said afterward. "I'm just really hooked on this TV show."

He seemed to be watching a televised high school wrestling match.

"Oh, that's okay," I said. "I'm supposed to take a shower now anyway." I stood in the doorway with my grocery bags for a few moments trying to think of something else to say that would make that statement seem less unbearably awkward, then closed the door and left, accepting failure.

Jono and I had sex again, a few weeks later, in my bedroom. He spent the night without being invited.

He passed Courtney in the kitchen as he left in the morning, where he tried to initiate some kind of secret handshake with her and then laughed at her when she didn't know the moves. She made a face to me that said, "What are you doing? This person is clearly a huge moron," and I made a face back at her that said, "Oh, what? Do you have something against mo- rons all of a sudden?" Then she made a face at me that said, "Go get 'em, I guess," and I made a face back to her that said, "Hahaha," and Jono kissed me and said, "See you later, babe," and I smiled at him and then gave Courtney a look that said, "Don't judge me for being emotionally irrespon-sible, shallow, and increasingly pathetic; this is the life I've chosen." And then Courtney yelled, "Nice to meet you," after Jono had already closed our front door.

I called Mickey several times after we broke up, asking to be forgiven for breaking up with him. He told me he didn't understand what I was trying to do and didn't think he should be around me.

"Please," I said. "Please be around me. Please just go to the movies with me. If I've ruined our relationship, I'll never be able to forgive myself."

At the theater, Mickey stood in line to buy popcorn and sodas while I reserved our seats. As I was waiting for Mickey, I sent a text to Jono that said, "what's up."

To this day, I am still waiting for a response.

Mickey tried to hold my hand during the previews and I said, "Stop," loud enough for several people to look over at us angrily. I looked back angrily at the people, knowing I would remember their faces in the future whenever I needed someone to blame for the downward spiral that was my life.

I handed the cashier at the taqueria a crumpled wad of un-counted bills to pay for my burrito and avoided eye contact with her while she flattened the bills, counted them, and handed the overage back to me.

The cashier could blame my mom for that one. My mom had tried to instill in me an overeager politeness to strangers and her gross boyfriends.

I rebelled against it, having nothing much else to rebel against.

I pity my mom just for the sheer satisfaction of knowing how irritated and defensive she'd be if she knew I was pitying her.

But I also get mad if she doesn't call before noon on my birthday.

I called Mickey. It seemed like he was irritated but trying to be patient. I felt irritated by his patience. Why did he pick up the phone if he didn't want to talk to me? Why didn't he delete my voicemail without listening to it? Why did he endure me?

"I want to talk," I said.

"I can't," he said. "I have to go to work."

My friend Jason was wearing a shirt that I had given to Mickey the year before.

It was a pink collared shirt, recognizable by the small drip of blue paint along the hem.

I knew that Jason didn't hang out with Mickey, and if he had then Jason definitely would have told me, so he must have gotten the shirt from Felix, who is their only mutual friend as far as I know, and who has given Jason clothing in the past.

Mickey must have intentionally given it to Felix, knowing Felix knew Jason and knowing Felix's predisposition to give away clothing. He had to know it was highly likely that I would see Jason wearing the shirt and deduce that Mickey had done this intentionally, ensuring that I would want to follow the life of the shirt. Mickey knew that once I had made these deductions I would, inevitably, feel somewhat crazy for projecting all of this scheming onto him, and maybe a little paranoid about my own sanity, and sick to my stomach for letting the sight of a shirt control my mood. But Mickey would also know I'd be happy that he was communicating with me at all, which meant that he either hated me or loved me but definitely did not feel nothing for me.

I am wearing the underwear Mickey gave to me as a joke, but I am not wearing them as a joke, which seems really funny.

Alexei started to tell me a story about his friend Pickle who I had supposedly met before, and I felt like an asshole for not remembering meeting this person even though I was pretty sure I had never met him, because I'm not sure how I could forget a name like Pickle.

Then there was a weird pause in Alexei's story and I couldn't remember what he had said before the pause, because I guess I wasn't fully listening. I didn't know how to respond, or if I was supposed to, so I laughed nervously, and hoped that laughing was the right thing to do.

I felt better when Alexei sort of laughed, too.

Courtney invited me to go to her friend Lucy's house to watch the season premiere of *America's Next Top Model*, but I didn't want to go because I was too horribly lonely to put myself in a social situation.

It shouldn't be assumed that I want to be a sympathetic character in the story of my life, because that would imply that my actions are designed to convey something that other people might find attractive or relatable instead of my actions having their own meaning, separate from others' interpretations of them.

I told Courtney I didn't want to go because I hadn't seen all the episodes of the previous season of *America's Next Top Model* and I didn't want to see any spoilers.

"You already know who won," Courtney said.

"Yeah, but I don't know how it all went down," I said.

I feel desperate to be by myself even when I'm already totally alone.

It feels like I am waiting for somebody to enter my life so I can immediately tell them to turn around and leave.

Like, "This isn't a fucking entrance."

I want my own artistic process to leave me alone. It is always making symbols of my feelings when it has not been invited to do so, saying, "Hey, this might be worth examining closely and at length. Maybe in charcoal?"

"Look at how you've flopped over on your bed with your leg over the footboard and your face smashed into that handwoven textile. It is symbolic of how our relationships with objects change as our moods change."

"What if you collected all the items in your bedroom that you've cried into, and display them under glass as art objects?"

"I bet people would be interested in seeing that."

I want to have an art show that is made up of big black words displayed on the white walls of the gallery.

During the show I want to stand around the gallery looking elegant and sad. I want everyone to have a deep desire to approach me but also a deep hesitancy. I want them to think, "She looks so elegant, I would just ruin her beauty by standing next to her."

All the pieces will be untitled, an homage to all the unnamed, misunderstood feelings that exist in the world.

Untitled #1

THIS IS NOT A METAPHOR FOR ANYTHING. PLEASE APPROACH THE ARTIST. SHE'S VERY LONELY.

Untitled #2

I'M TERRIFIED THAT DEEP DOWN INSIDE I'M NOT THAT
INTERESTING AND I'M TERRIFIED THAT EVERYONE AL-
READY KNOWS.

"We have to let you go," my boss said.

"Let go," I said back to him. Then I chuckled.

I thought laughter would help make me appear confident, as if I could make my boss feel insubordinate.

It wasn't the lack of a paycheck that made me nervous, but the idea that I would no longer have to ride a bus forty-five minutes to an office that perpetually smelled like the inside of a microwave, to sit for eight hours organizing digital files and sending emails to my coworkers attempting to clarify a specific line item on a receipt, before riding the bus again for forty-five minutes, and then walking home in the dark.

My boss looked at me with pity. "You've been checking out," he said.

"No, no," I said. "I would never do that."

"Your performance is slipping and I need a tight crew around here."

"Of course," I said.

On the bus ride home, I expected something to happen to indicate that something was indeed happening, but nothing like that happened.

The bus driver was somewhat pleasant, which seemed somewhat unusual, I guess. The other riders listened to their headphones and politely ignored me.

I imagined the bus getting stuck in a tunnel during an earthquake. The earth surrounding the tunnel would fall all around the bus, trapping me, the driver, and the five other passengers within it. We would be stuck down there for days or weeks before the rescue team would be able to get to us. Our iPods would be dead by then. We would be forced to talk to one another.

I picked out the person on the bus who I would be drawn to initially, and then I picked the second person that I would be drawn to after the first person inevitably turned out to be an idiot. I would ask the second person questions about his life. I would be bored by his life history, but I would consider falling in love with him for the sake of the story.

We met while we were trapped on a bus in a tunnel for twenty-four days. We all thought we were going to die. I happened to have fruit snacks in my bag because I had been fired from my job that day and had to clean out my desk. I had kept those fruit snacks in my desk for over a year. They were the fruit snacks that saved our lives. We fell madly in love.

When I got home after being fired I made a salad bigger than any person could ever eat in one sitting, watched clips of *What Not To Wear* on YouTube, and earnestly considered sending photos of myself and my ratty wardrobe to the show's producers.

I imagined my big reveal at the end of the show, when I would show my family and loved ones my new look, complete with hair and makeup. I would walk out into the center of a rented restaurant and spin around in an exaggerated way, smiling stupidly, like I knew I was on television and felt kind of sarcastic about it.

"You look great," everyone would say, "But we love you for who you are. We loved your old overalls and clogs. But don't get us wrong—you look great now, too!"

I didn't recognize their faces, but they looked like good people.

I typed "what not to wear casting" into a search engine.

There were probably many reasons that I wouldn't have ended up on the show, the most reasonable of which was that the show had been cancelled for a couple of years.

I guess you don't know what you've got 'til it's gone.

"Let go," was how my boss put it, as if I were Mariah Carey's beloved butterfly that might come back to work one day.

I was free at last from the salary plus benefits that bound me. Free at last to eat the remainder of last night's noodles over the stovetop.

Free at last to buy a garlic press online at 3:00 a.m. while stoned, after determining that I have a psychic connection with Gordon Ramsay.

Free at last to spend over two hours shaving my bikini line when I know I'm going to be wearing the same thermal pants for the next ten days.

Free at last to conceptualize a video game where you have to spread the gossip about some guy named Tim quickly enough so that the gossip saturates the community before Tim figures out that you are the one spreading gossip.

Free at last to read all 296 comments under a YouTube video of a baby and a dog watching TV together.

I kissed Alexei when I was really drunk one night, but it took so long to get past kissing that by the time his hands started moving around my body in a way that could not be interpreted as accidental I was only partially drunk, and by the time our clothes came off I was sober enough to know that I didn't really want my clothes off, but they were already off so I decided not to be too hard on myself about it.

In the morning he bought me a breakfast burrito. It seemed like he intended the gesture to be cruel, like, "Is this all I have to do to get you to not talk shit about me to your dumb friends? Buy you a burrito?"

I guess I find it charming to be around people who act like they don't care at all what I think.

I guess I've chosen to perceive someone's total lack of effort as a deep, very real need to be liked by me.

Alexei took me to a show opening for an artist he had been friends with in college. Alexei looked at each of the paintings for what seemed like exactly one minute, avoided making eye contact with anybody, and then walked to the snack table to eat chips dipped evenly in salsa.

There were several important-looking people standing around the artist, who looked slightly too happy and well-adjusted for the art world.

I looked around at some of the work. I mostly liked it, but it was the type of art that seemed like it was made by someone I might hate, so I didn't spend too long looking at or seeming to appreciate any particular thing and decided to wait until Alexei introduced me to the artist to determine my opinion.

Alexei told me we needed to get on the train to go home as soon as possible, and that there was literally no time to say hello to anyone. I had seen the artist look over at Alexei several times, but he had been engaged in conversation with other people at the show.

We went to Alexei's apartment and watched almost the entire second season of *The Office* on Netflix and passed out without having sex. It felt intimate on a level that was overwhelming to me.

I didn't call him again for two weeks, and when I finally called he didn't ask why I hadn't called and didn't seem to notice that any time had passed.

Having total control over when I talk to him comes in handy. I can imagine myself falling in love with him for only that reason.

I don't know if I'm dating Alexei. Or if Alexei thinks he's dating me.

Or if he kind of thinks we're dating but is searching for confirmation in my actions or words.

Or if he confidently thinks we're dating, and has already told his close friends and relatives that he has a girlfriend.

I don't know if I want to be his girlfriend, or if I just like sleeping with him, or if I even like sleeping with him.

Maybe I sleep with Alexei because it helps me believe there is some reason for me to be on this Earth.

Maybe the only thing I like about sex is the existential validation.

Without the daily structure of a long list of seemingly random tasks governed by a force I willingly gave up power to, I am lost in time. Time has become meaningless in a bad way.

No, a good way.

"Don't Hot Cheetos give you heartburn?" I asked the abyss.

"There's no way to ever know," the abyss answered. "You can't afford that shit."

But the abyss was wrong, because I had food stamps.

"You can't use food stamps for Hot Cheetos," the abyss said.

"Yeah, you can," I said.

I was in high spirits because I had just been fired from my job and had forced myself to be in high spirits.

I showed up at my mom's house, ready to apologize for showing up without calling first. I hadn't talked to my mom in months for what seemed like no reason.

A tiny Asian man opened her door and I said, "Mom," at him. "I mean, my mom," I clarified. "Where is she?"

He called a tiny Asian woman over, who said she didn't speak English.

I called my mom from the car and got her voicemail: "Hi, this is Diane, leave a message." I had heard it hundreds of times before.

My message went, "Dearest Mother, I am merely inquiring as to your whereabouts. Haven't seen you, where are you? Also, who is in your house? Call me back at your earliest convenience. Thank you."

The first few times I called my mom after finding out she had moved, I felt angry and annoyed. I left short, curt messages on her voicemail, like, "Hello, it's me, okay, bye."

The next few times I called, I felt confused and worried in a passive aggressive way. I left short, demanding messages on her voicemail, like, "Hi, haven't heard from you. Call me right away so I know if you've been kidnapped by a cult or not."

The last time I called, I felt sarcastic and conflicted in a defensive and vulnerable way, and didn't leave a voicemail.

One day, I texted her from Alexei's phone. "Diane. How are you?"

She immediately replied, "New phone. Who is this?"

I texted my name.

Fifty-five minutes later she responded, "Good. And you?"

"Pretty good. What are your plans for the Fourth of July?"

She didn't text back.

Untitled #3

THE FACT THAT MY LIFE IS WORTHLESS AND EMBARRASS-
ING IS WHAT MAKES MY ART INTERESTING.

OR IS IT THE OTHER WAY AROUND?

Untitled #4

WE MAY HAVE GOTTEN AHEAD OF OURSELVES.

THIS ISN'T ART UNTIL SOMEONE HAS PAID FOR IT.

My phone broke the way phones always break: I threw it against something.

I lost all my contact information, so I can't call or text my mom again unless I ask someone for her phone number or otherwise humiliate myself.

I can see on her Facebook profile—which I accessed through a fake account that I made exclusively to look at my mom's profile because she blocked me from viewing it on my regular account—that she had recently seen *The Joy Luck Club*.

She had posted a vague but impassioned status update a few days before: "I just want to take a minute to say thank you to everyone who has stayed by my side the last few months. I know now who my friends are and who has just used me to get ahead in their own lives! Watch out for the users and losers in your life, they will ask for your love and support and then not be there for you when you need it. And if they don't love you when you need it most, then they don't love you at all. That's my two cents!"

I wasn't sure if the post was about me.

If it was, it could not have been written in hopes that I would see it, since she blocked my account.

If the status was about me but wasn't meant for me to read, then who was it for? Her friends from high school? Her AA sponsor? The people who send her coins for Candy Crush or whatever? Why was it important to her for these people to know that someone betrayed her?

In another post she talked about how rewarding it was to have a garden. There was also a long post that referenced Shakira, Jon Stewart, and her "faith in humanity."

I thought the posts were maybe a code I had to decipher.

But I checked, and there's no way that "faith in humanity" is an acrostic poem.

I woke up after blacking out and saw that I had written NOT EVERYTHING IS A METAPHOR on my left arm and IMPORTANT INFORMATION ON OTHER ARM on my right arm.

It must be so disgusting to watch something that was once a part of yourself slowly turn into something so separate and opinionated.

Like watching your left arm detach from your body and go to college in Santa Cruz to study gender politics and practice polyamory. Things you never planned for your arm, things that are so out of your range of understanding you hadn't even thought to warn the arm against them.

I can imagine looking at photographs of the arm when it was younger and feeling panicky about the swiftness with which life passes a person.

How do you have a conversation about gender politics with an arm that thinks for itself? I can imagine wondering, while mentally suppressing the much more important question, *What is gender politics?*

I can understand feeling helpless and angry that the arm didn't acquire the values you thought were embedded into your flesh.

I can imagine wanting to disown the arm, overconfident and argumentative about its decisions, constantly making you feel old and foolish when you ask simple questions about its life. I can imagine wanting to focus once again on yourself, on the other arm and the few other appendages that haven't de-tached from you, that seem to still find you interesting and knowledgeable and worth being connected to.

I can imagine trying to forget about the arm.

If I had been asked three years ago, "Do you put family first?" I would have been confused by the question. I have never been in the habit of making proclamations about what I did or did not "put first," and asking me a question like that would have made me feel unfairly confronted.

Actually, it would have probably seemed like the question was trying to make me feel guilty before I even had time to answer.

Like, it's just worded in a really judgmental way or something. Or implies that obviously we should all be putting our families first before anything else no matter what.

Before ourselves.

Before any other people, because it is unacceptable that we care about other people more than our family.

Even if there's no evidence that our family puts us first.

Or, if they do, that they will for very long.

But how do you tell that to a question?

I walked around the lake listening to The Shins. If I happened to run into Mickey, and he happened to ask me what I was listening to (which he almost certainly would because that is exactly the kind of thing he is interested in), I would say The Shins. It would be implied that I had been thinking of him while walking around the lake, because he had given me my first Shins album, and we had listened to it together frequently. It would be an overt implication, and possible only because of the psychic connection I had always felt we had.

Mickey called me before the first track on the album ended, before I had even reached the part of the lake where I usually sit and watch ducks for a few minutes before opening my sketchbook. Given that we hadn't talked on the phone recently, or talked much in any capacity in the last few months, it was safe to assume he had taken a few minutes to decide to call me before he pressed Send on his phone and the call went through. It was that same couple of minutes wherein I had been contemplating our accidental meeting at the lake and our hypothetical conversation about The Shins.

In any case, it proved my point about our psychic connection. "Hello? Mickey?"

I heard the faint, muffled rustling of fabric and a long, intentional sniff.

"Mickey," I said again. I had been pocket dialed. I listened to the interior of his pocket or hand or backpack or whatever for almost a minute before realizing that he would be able to see the duration of the call, and hung up.

When I hung up my phone started playing The Shins again, only my earphones weren't plugged in anymore so the music came from the phone's speaker. I was mortified at the fact that the people around me at the lake would not understand the context of my music choice, even though the only people around were two handyman-looking people and a group of ducks.

I keep telling myself that what I am going through now could be compared to a breakup, even though what I am going through is precisely a breakup.

Thinking about how tough and strong I am brings me to tears more easily than thinking about how vulnerable and small I am.

With $313.56 in my bank account and no plans of acquiring any new money in the foreseeable future, I spent $84.00 enrolling in a six-week ceramics class, clay and tools included. I thought I needed a hobby separate from myself and from my "real" art practice. I wanted to see what else my hands could do. I wanted to listen to the elderly women who enrolled in the class as they casually talked about estrogen. I wanted to arrive late to each session, rudely and unapologetically, so that the elderly students and the elderly woman who taught the course would know I was a total badass. I wanted to make small coil pots.

I made more than sixty coil pots. I spent twenty dollars on a blue speckled glaze and eleven dollars on a pale yellow glaze. I carved my last name into the bottom of my coil pots before firing them.

An elderly woman named Grace was the star of our class. She threw thin, even pots on the wheel and glazed them with care and precision, if not much originality. She was well loved by the students in our class, who sat at tables near the potter's wheels and watched her work.

"She has nice craftsmanship but she is not an artist," I thought to myself, smoothing the rim on what would end up being a blue-speckled, intentionally lopsided, highbrow Q-tip holder for my shared bathroom. "I take artistic risks with my small coil pots that neither Grace nor any of the other women in this class will ever know how to appreciate."

The last time I talked to my mom I didn't know it would be the last time, so perhaps I acted cold towards her.

I wish I could remember my exact tone of voice, or the exact phrasing of what I said.

I asked for a pair of heels that she had borrowed over a year earlier. She threw them to me one at a time.

Neither of us has ever been good at talking about our feelings, but she was the one who had failed to return my shoes so I wasn't exactly eager to make her feel good about it.

I noticed some damage on the shoes and pointed it out to her. She said something like, "They're just shoes," which seems symbolic now.

Maybe she was trying to tell me that I blow things out of proportion.

Maybe that's why she won't return my calls.

I am willing myself to have a manic episode just so I can get out of bed today.

I have preemptively left tabs open in my browser showing web results for "Henry Darger" and "are octopuses smart" in case I die today and someone wants to know how interesting I was.

"When I was about sixteen," I said, "there was a knock on our door. A small boy came over because his parents were fighting and he was scared. He must have been a neighbor boy but we didn't recognize him. My mom asked him if he had any other relatives in town that might come pick him up, and he said he had a grandma but he didn't know her phone number."

"That's kind of weird," said Courtney. She was slicing carrots on the cutting board.

"My mom didn't want to call the police because she understood that people sometimes have fights and she didn't want to be responsible for one of his parents going to jail. But she didn't want to send the boy back to his house because if something happened to him, she would feel responsible. And she didn't want to keep the boy in our house because it seemed inappropriate. While we were deciding what to do, his mom just walked into our apartment, grabbed the boy and they left."

"What?" Courtney said, somewhat distractedly.

I felt self-conscious and embarrassed for talking so much, and somewhat sad that I felt self-conscious and embarrassed about wanting to talk to my roommate. Then I realized I was lonely and had very few people to talk to, which made me feel like something was wrong with me that I couldn't identify and fix. That problem, whatever it was, was what had made it difficult for me, all my life, to make and keep friends.

Then I realized that I'd actually had plenty of great relationships of all kinds, many that I was still maintaining and that I honestly considered healthy, and it was ridiculous to believe, even if only for a couple of seconds, that I literally had no friends in the world when I so clearly did. I almost felt compelled to list them, just to prove it to myself.

"Never mind," I said, and got up to go to my room.

"Do you want salad?" she said.

"No, thanks," I said at a volume she would have had a hard time hearing even if she had been listening carefully, and then accidentally slammed my door.

Untitled #5

MAYBE SOME LOVE STORIES HAVE UNHAPPY ENDINGS
AND UNHAPPY MIDDLES AND UNHAPPY BEGINNINGS
AND MAYBE THEY WERE NEVER REALLY ABOUT LOVE
AND NEVER REALLY GOT AROUND TO TELLING A STORY
BUT MAYBE THAT'S OKAY AND WE CAN ALL MOVE ON
FROM IT KNOWING THAT WE DID THE BEST WE COULD.

Alexei came to the opening of a group show I was part of in San Francisco. I regretted inviting him, and couldn't remember why I had.

I begrudgingly introduced him to a couple of my art acquaintances while wishing he would leave. He followed me around while I talked to people, and refilled my cup with wine when I asked him to.

"I have to stay here for a while," I said. "But I can meet up later if you want."

"Okay. Do you want to get dinner?" Alexei said.

"Yeah," I said, but I went out to dinner with the gallery owner and some of the other artists instead, and didn't call him or text him for the next month.

I can see that I could easily make Alexei my boyfriend.

And I can also see that we don't think much of each other.

I prefer to keep him at arm's reach, where I can pull him in or push him away with the same amount of effort.

I don't like spending time with Alexei, but I also don't like not having anyone to sleep with when I feel like it.

I caught myself trying to remember my first interaction with my mom and then remembered that I once lived in her body.

That I had spent weeks there without her knowing, thinking maybe she was experiencing a particularly weird case of ovulation.

My body was indistinguishable from her flesh until I was born, at which point, as she described it, I was more important to her than her self.

Untitled #6

PART OF APPRECIATING ART IS LOOKING AWAY FROM
THE ART WHILE STILL THINKING ABOUT IT.

I think I look more beautiful when Courtney and I are together. She's prettier than I am, but only by a little, and I think that dynamic adds to my attractiveness.

I think what happens is that, instead of appearing to be one attractive female and one slightly less attractive female, we are rounded up to Two Attractive Females. Therefore, it is in my best interest for her to continue being beautiful, because when she has a large zit or wears a particularly careless outfit, it brings us down as a unit.

Furthermore, it is not worth the effort to put any energy into my looks when I am going to hang out with Courtney, as she will bring my projected attractiveness level up anyway. If I increase my attractiveness, it will increase the attractiveness of us as a unit and, though we will attract more attention that way, she will always be the main recipient of that attention because she is always prettier than I am, even if only slightly, and it will be she who benefits from the extra effort I expended.

If Courtney, however, decides to expend extra energy on her appearance before hanging out with me, thereby increasing our attractiveness as a unit, I will benefit from that more than I if I had been the one to expend the extra energy on my appearance. Because even though Courtney looks more beautiful than usual and the gap between my beauty and hers has widened, I am still second to her beauty (as I always have been). Being second most attractive to an exceedingly beautiful girl is objectively better than being second most attractive to a beautiful girl.

"I like your shirt," I said.

"I know," Alexei said. "You like vintage fabrics and bright colors. I know. I get it."

Alexei said, "Have you ever made a sandcastle?"

"Yeah," I said. "I used to make them all the time with my cousin and uncle."

Alexei said, "No, like a really professional looking sandcastle. Like with special sandcastle techniques."

I said, "Yeah, my family met this guy on the beach one time who taught us some cool sandcastle tricks. He had all these little tools, too, for making stairs look really symmetrical and whatever."

Alexei said, "No. You know what I'm saying. You, by yourself, have never made a really nice, big, professional-looking sandcastle, like you would see in a magazine about the beach or something."

"I don't know. I think I'm pretty good at making sandcastles."
"Jesus Christ."

For a while, I had been working on a series of drawings made up of dots inside of small circles, thousands of dots, in no particular pattern or design, on large sheets of expensive paper. I spent whole days on these drawings, focusing on the word "spend" as I did them. I told myself I was "spending" my life on an abstract pointless gesture. I hoped that by acknowledging that I had voluntarily created an abstract, pointless activity for myself, I was making a comment about the fleetingness of life and the disconnect between what we thought of as important versus what we thought of as a waste of time.

I hoped to get a gallery show of these drawings and find some way to use the word "spend" to discuss my work.

"The idea was to spend my time. Each hour I spent could get me two hundred to three hundred dots."

Something like that.

I planned to make fifty or sixty of them—it would take me ten years to do it—and then I would put the drawings in one room and look around and see the last ten years of my life displayed on the walls.

I would say, "I traded those years of my life for ten to twelve drawings."

Unfortunately, the drawings were beautiful, so conceptually my drawings didn't work. Brains are trained to find patterns in the world, connect dots to make lines, see lines as implications of objects, relate to objects in a way that suits their preconceived ideas about themselves. Patterns emerged from the dots and lines even though I was forcing my hand not to make any. A dot can't just be a dot if it is surrounded by other dots. It was embarrassing, and I stopped working on the drawings.

Later, I saw the same sort of dot pattern drawings in a gallery and felt humiliated at how smart I thought my own dot paintings were.

Anything can be humiliating, but sometimes I think that making art is a uniquely humiliating experience. For your work to be successful, it has to possess or imply original thought (which is impossible), intelligence (which is dependent on the intelligence of other people and, therefore, uncontrollable), or visual appeal (which is pointless and stupid and demeaning).

I tried to embrace my trashiness for a long time before realizing that embracing one's trashiness is probably super highbrow.

But maybe it's trashy of me to assume that an awareness of the signifiers of your class is highbrow.

Although creating an elaborate explanation for why you might be considered trashy in an effort to actually seem highbrow does seem trashy.

To be honest, I'd be lucky if either side wanted me.

Is self-deprecation highbrow or lowbrow?

Let me say that I buy into any theory that minimizes my obligations in life, especially regarding controlling my own behavior or taking responsibility for my actions. I also buy into anything that encourages others to regard my bad behavior as important and vital to a culturally diverse community.

I don't know, we're all miserable, right? So why not allow me to blame myself?

I opened the front door for Alexei, who briefly smiled while waiting for me to move out of the way of the doorway so he could enter without obstacle.

He said, "I'm tired."

I said, "But we were planning on working in our sketchbooks tonight."

"Well, I'm too tired. I want to cuddle and go to sleep."

"I invited Courtney and her friend Slick to hang out with us. Courtney is making us drinks right now."

Alexei didn't say anything but aggressively pulled his over-sized sketchbook from his messenger bag, threw himself onto the couch, and immediately began work on what seemed like, based only on his attentiveness and the proximity of his face to the sketchbook, very fine detail work.

"Who wants extra lime in their mojito?" Courtney called from the kitchen.

Alexei didn't look up and didn't say anything, but he widened his eyes and slowed his movements to imply conscious control of his body, which is, I think, the universal code for "I'd rather be in fucking hell."

I yelled, "We both want extra lime," in the most cheerful voice I could manage without sounding sarcastic, and smiled maliciously at Alexei, who looked at me like I was the girl at the checkout counter that one time who asked if he had found everything he was looking for when the only item he was purchasing was Gushing Grape Hubba Bubba Bubble Tape because it was the only gum he could find and he was too insecure in his masculinity to ask where the normal gum was.

Alexei said he was offended by some of the brainless comments that certain celebrities have made about wealth distribution and race. When I asked him what in particular offended him, he said that it was offensive that the resources of our Earth are being wasted on the silly meaningless whims of attractive, well-connected idiots. I was impressed because he doesn't usually speak in such long sentences.

"I get that people don't want to look old, but I think some people go too far with makeup and plastic surgery."

I said, "I think so, too. Feeling comfortable with yourself is sexy."

Alexei said, "I'm not talking about sexy, it's just like, come on, you look like a weird freak."

I said, "Well, I think people do it to feel sexy. They don't want to look old and unattractive. They want to look young and they want their skin to be tight and stuff. Because marketing and things like that are designed to make people feel unsexy." Alexei said, "It's not about sexiness. It's just totally unrealistic."

I said, "You think there's a big difference between wanting to be attractive and wanting to be sexy?"

Alexei said, "You're not listening and it's super annoying."

Mickey's hair is probably still growing out from that awful haircut I gave him.

I sent Alexei a text message that said, "I'm pissed."

I had gone shopping for a new scarf and had run into someone I had kind of known five or six years prior and was forced
to briefly speak with them. I wasn't actually pissed, but I knew
it was within my right to be pissed.

Alexei texted back, "Big surprise," without asking me what I
was pissed about.

I want to understand Courtney's motivation in life, but I feel like I have to turn off the parts of my brain I like the most in order to turn on the parts of my brain that help me understand her.

Courtney said, "Should I wear this skirt or the red one?"

I said, "The red one."

She put on the red one. "I can't actually wear this. I feel like a slut."

I said, "No, you look like a weird nerd."

"Even with these boots?"

"I don't like the skirt. Sorry, I should have asked if I could be honest before I said that."

She said, "I'll try on something else."

"I like the shirt, though," I said. She took it off and threw it to me and told me to keep it.

I put on the shirt and noticed a gross brown stain that had been hidden more effectively by the shadow of Courtney's breasts, which were larger and more shadow producing than mine.

I considered wearing the shirt to my next job interview.

Mickey randomly texted and asked if I wanted to get coffee. "YES!!!" I responded, having just described my mood to Courtney as "exuberant."

Consciously, I didn't want to hurt Mickey, but believing that I didn't want to hurt Mickey suddenly felt like some larger effort to hurt Mickey more deeply and profoundly than I had ever hurt him before.

I wanted him to beg to be hurt by me, so that when I hurt him it would be completely his fault, and I would be the blameless agent of his pain who would wipe his tears away from his face and say, "Well, why did you make the wounds so deep if you didn't think you could handle it?"

I considered talking to Mickey about this, but I didn't think he would understand. I kept thinking, "Mickey isn't hot enough to understand," even though I considered Mickey extremely attractive.

When we had coffee I acted cold toward him in an effort to derail my own plan (which was to wait for him to offer his love to me, opening himself up for my demented but blame-less puppy kicking, at which point, instead of kicking him like he was begging for, I had decided somewhat last minute that I would refuse to offer the pain he was opening himself up to as a means of further entrapping him in my increasingly fucked up manipulation game). But he mistook my coldness for sadness and tried to comfort me.

"I don't want to mislead you," I said. "I don't want a boyfriend right now."

"Wow. Fascinating," Mickey said. "I was hoping we could arbitrarily jump to that topic with no segue."

But he was right. I was sad.

I told Mickey I didn't want a boyfriend, but I immediately started acting girlfriend-y.

I sent him texts that held no useful information, sometimes just an emoji.

I definitely noticed if he didn't answer my texts in a timely fashion.

I thought about him when I hung out with other people.

If we weren't hanging out one night, I wanted to know what he was doing instead.

After a few weeks, Mickey said, "What are we doing?"

I said, "I'm pretending to give you a stick-and-poke of a gallon of milk."

I looked into Mickey's eyes and blinked super casually a few times. If someone had been recording just my eyes, you might guess that I was watching TV, standing in line at the grocery store, or trying to remember what I ate for breakfast. I looked at one of his eyes, then the other, allowing my own eyelids to droop slightly as if I had heavy makeup on and it was exhausting to hold my eyes open. But I couldn't help it, and finally I smiled.

I received a text from my friend Gina that said, "I ran into your mom at the Safeway on Pleasant Valley."

I texted my mom immediately to ask, "How are you doing?"

I texted Gina, "Did you say hello?" and she texted back, "Yeah, she seemed confused, I don't think she remembered me. What are you up to?"

I didn't respond to Gina.

Instead, I wrote a second text to my mom, even though the first text remained unanswered, saying, "What are you doing in my neighborhood?" But I didn't send it and I didn't erase it. I let the message sit in my text box.

Periodically I opened our conversation and saw my message still waiting there, unsent.

My favorite memory is when I was five and tried to convince my mom that *she* was the one who smeared finger paint all over my bedroom windows.

Untitled #7

I AM SURE THAT ONE DAY I WILL BE A GREAT ARTIST.

I'LL BE SO SUCCESSFUL THAT YOU'LL BE AFRAID TO TALK
TO ME.

AND I'LL STILL BE AFRAID TO TALK TO YOU, TOO.

I've thought about making a series of drawings of my mom's face and showing them in either a popular gallery or maybe somewhere close to where she lives, so that she would definitely see it or hear about it and be forced to angrily contact me to suggest I go to hell or something, which would at least be dialogue.

I would want to say, "I'm your child." But instead I would say, "This series is an attempt at real honesty unfiltered by my moral responsibilities. These images of your face are my weapons against you. What does it mean for a viewer to be in a room full of the weapons a woman has created to use against her mother?"

Untitled #8

OPEN YOUR EYES HALFWAY AND LOOK DIRECTLY AND UNFLINCHINGLY AT THAT WHICH YOU FEEL MOST JUDGED BY AND IT WILL PROBABLY GO AWAY.

I LEARNED THAT TRICK IN HIGH SCHOOL.

Untitled #9

PLEASE TAKE CARE OF THIS WORK OF ART WHEN YOU
TAKE IT HOME TONIGHT IN YOUR THOUGHTS.

MAYBE YOU BELIEVE THAT BECAUSE IT ONLY EXISTS IN
YOUR THOUGHTS YOU DON'T NEED TO TAKE CARE
OF IT.

PLEASE TRY TO DISREGARD THAT THOUGHT.

I love the calm, rational voices that cooking show hosts use to describe food, those gentle reminders to cook a chicken corpse thoroughly before pouring your favorite delicate sauce over it.

Cooking show hosts, it seems, have little confidence in the common sense levels of their viewers.

Sometimes there are some pretty good segments on sauces. Cream sauces. Tomato sauces. Gravy, even. Ugly, complicated, demanding sauces originating in places that even the host can't pronounce.

I'm going to make a sauce that is an ode to getting out of the house. The sauce will be my masterwork. It will be cream based.

"I thought the sauce was about depression," I'll say to the art critics. "But the sauce didn't want to be about depression. This sauce is about getting out and living your life and following your dreams. In reality, this sauce was never about depression. It never could have been. The sauce had its own voice. It wanted to speak, and I was the medium from which it could do so. In this way, I am the art, and the sauce is the artist. I am this sauce's lifework. It incorporates basil but it is not a pesto."

I have gone through hundreds of job listings at a rapid pace. I've started skimming them for keywords that would make them deal breakers, things like "full time," or "some weekends," or "long-term," or "fast-paced environment," so that I wouldn't waste my time reading the full ad for a job I would never apply for.

But I noticed that I also skimmed for words like "friendly," and "polite," as if I could never imagine using those adjectives to describe myself.

You can't put those things on your resume, so how do you convince someone you possess those qualities? You either are friendly and polite or you act friendly and polite.

But acting is outside of my range of expertise.

When Mickey was at work I painted a window onto his bedroom wall. The window was asymmetrical and lopsided and kind of too small and not in a good place on the wall for a window.

At first I painted a view of a rolling vineyard, but then I painted curtains over the window. Thick, red curtains with purple ties that pulled the curtains back to show a sliver of the rolling vineyard.

I took the art that Mickey had on the wall and moved it to the other three walls, so that this wall could just have the window.

Mickey laughed when he came home. He wasn't worried about any of the things I expected him to be worried about. He liked the window.

I was thinking about the benefits of eating in-season produce because I had just read *The Omnivore's Dilemma*. The book sort of makes an argument for eating local, in-season produce because it leaves a smaller carbon footprint. It could also be healthier for a person, theoretically, if one lives in the same general area as their ancestors, because one would be eating some of the same foods one's ancestors would have eaten, and one's body may have evolved to handle the in-season produce more effectively than produce that has been flown in from another country.

Grapes were in season.

Whenever I buy grapes I end up not eating them. I imagine myself as someone who likes grapes, but I am actually someone who does not like grapes and who does not eat grapes when she buys them.

While I was thinking all of this, Mickey, who was clipping his toenails on the other side of the room, said, "You're not a big fruit person, are you?"

I felt incredibly close to Mickey in that moment. I felt like he could intuitively understand the trajectory of my mind, or was connected to me in some transcendent way, breaking down one of the many barriers that made us two separate people instead of one whole.

But I could never know what Mickey thought or felt, despite occasional reassurances. It felt the same as the way I couldn't know if, when I held his hand for comfort while we fell asleep, he felt comforted, too, or was merely patiently attending to my embarrassing emotional needs. Our emotional vocabularies didn't seem to be sufficient enough to relay this kind of information.

"Say that you love me," I said as I put two plates of eggs on the table for us.

"I love you," said Mickey.

"How do you know you love me?"

"I love you. It's not complicated."

"How do you know that what you are experiencing is not just a flood of serotonin?"

"If it's a flood of serotonin, then you're causing the flood."

"You don't know that. You can't know if you love me, because you don't have the capability to understand your own brain."

"Okay, but that would mean that nobody loves anybody."

"Yeah, love is just . . . unrealistic," I said.

"Well, do you love me?"

The eggs we made, while technically well executed, were getting cold on the table between us while we were arguing. I became increasingly worried about the temperature of the eggs, and I guessed that Mickey, based on how intently he was staring at them, was worrying about it as well.

"Yes. [But the truth is that if you weren't here] I [would] love [somebody else. And If my love isn't specific to] you [how can that really be love?]," I said.

"Well, I'm convinced [that you're totally fucking crazy]," he said.

We started eating. The eggs were still really good.

There should be a service to connect people with researchers who can help them study themselves. It would be marketed as a way of learning new things about oneself, and targeted at artists (who are generally self-absorbed and into the kind of thing that revolves completely around them) as a way to improve their art.

My mom loved Rob Thomas, the singer of Matchbox 20, more than any other man or beast on this earth. She didn't say it like that, but it sounds like something she'd say if she were trying to be funny while implying a sort of sarcasm regarding her feelings for Rob Thomas.

I've caught myself deciding to call her and ask if she thinks of me when she sings "how's it gonna be when you're not around," and then I realize that I don't have her phone number or any other contact information, and that what is actually playing is Third Eye Blind, and that I don't actually know the name of the lead singer of Third Eye Blind.

I asked Mickey if he ever ate cheese behind my back. He thought I was trying to frame him for eating cheese behind my back, but Mickey doesn't seem to know what it means to "frame" someone. We didn't go into all that. I said I just wanted to know if he abstained from cheese because I was abstaining from cheese, or if he ate cheese without telling me to protect my feelings, which would be gentlemanly.

Mickey said he didn't trust me, and that he couldn't remember whether or not he ate the cheese. The way he said, "the cheese," as if he were referring to a specific cheese he came into contact with, seemed to incriminate him.

But I guess I was just trying to prove that he is a gentleman.

I am punishing my neighbors for blasting the same Nelly Furtado song in a loop all week by blasting the same Nelly Furtado song in a loop from the living room. We'll see how long they can stand this shit.

It doesn't make evolutionary sense for humans to develop a defense against people who blast bass-y music from their apartments, because this kind of annoying behavior does not affect the reproductive tendencies of those affected by this annoying behavior, so it would be a waste of genetic energy.

But if this annoying behavior is attractive to people of the opposite sex, even just a few, then it is worth it to blast the bass-y music, even though it is annoying to many.

In this sense, annoying people who blast bass-y music from their annoying, stupid cars are winning the arms race against normal, everyday people who are annoyed by this behavior.

Untitled #10

CLOSE YOUR EYES AND IMAGINE YOU ARE AT HOME IN A RELAXED AND COMFORTABLE POSITION.

NOW IMAGINE A STRAY BULLET ENTERING YOUR HOME AND BLOWING THROUGH A 2-LITER SODA BOTTLE SITTING BESIDE YOU. IMAGINE THE LIQUID PULSING FROM THE BULLET HOLE ONTO THE FLOOR. YOU DON'T FEEL RELAXED AT ALL ANYMORE. YOU FEEL TERRIFIED.

YOU FEEL THE MOST AFRAID YOU HAVE EVER FELT, BUT ALL YOU CAN THINK IS, "THERE IS SODA SPILLING ONTO MY FLOOR."

NOW OPEN YOUR EYES AND TELL ME WHAT TIME I SHOULD COME OVER TONIGHT.

In some hypothetical future in which I have plenty of money and some form of public notoriety, when my mom calls me out of the blue, I won't answer.

And when she leaves a voicemail making her case for some portion of my money, I will listen to it several times, trying to believe that this is a person I once lived inside of, but I won't call her back.

If she calls again and leaves another voicemail, no matter what she says or what her tone of voice is when she says it, I will text her, asking only where I should send a check.

Then I will send a check for an amount larger than what she asked for, and she will feel pathetic and petty but happy to have some of my money, and I will feel manipulative and gross but happy to share my money with her.

And in that way I will feel close to her again.

I didn't want to go to Courtney's gallery opening.

Courtney wanted me to go and I said I would but, when the time came, I didn't want to go anymore.

I had seen all her work. I had talked to her at length about each piece. I had been honest with her about my feelings on her work. I pointed things out that could be corrected or worked through more thoroughly.

She had ignored every piece of advice I had given.

I could not be expected to stand in a room and tell her the show was great when I had already told her that I thought it needed work.

She sensed that I felt hesitant to go and she told me that it was important to her that I go. She said she wanted me there and that she needed my support.

I said that I couldn't go because I was sick. Courtney believed me because she knew only a truly selfish asshole would pretend to be sick after her roommate and *best friend* made it clear how important her attendance was at her gallery opening.

But it was in Courtney's best interest to believe that I was not a truly selfish asshole, because the implications that such a belief would have about Courtney's self worth (seeing as how she spent so much time with me, chose to live with me, etc.) were too terrible for someone like her to face.

I thought I saw myself on TV, but it was just an average look-ing blonde girl in a McDonalds commercial looking really self-satisfied about ordering McNuggets. Her image made me briefly but intensely believe that it was I who loved McNuggets. A moment later I realized that it wasn't me in the commercial and that, by extension, it wasn't me who loved McNuggets.

"But I *do* love McNuggets," I thought, confused somehow. I stared at the TV, which had moved on to present images promoting some new and improved way of making websites.

I feel like I had been tricked into relating to, then feeling alienated from, and then being enraptured by a product that normally I felt pretty indifferent about, which felt both reliev-ing and sad, like Big Brother's triumph in *1984* (spoilers).

Idea:

A film that shows two people's interactions with each other over the course of ten years.

I'm not sure what their relationship would be. Maybe they are coworkers. Or maybe one is the teacher of the other's child. Something intimate, yet formal. Their conversations are mostly about this shared interest.

But there is some kind of tension beneath the surface—a budding romantic relationship, or one is the other's drug dealer, or they want to be friends, but that's kind of an awkward thing to accomplish as an adult.

I guess that would be the job of the film to uncover. I don't have all the answers.

Being unemployed feels like being in *The Sims'* Build Mode, but with less soothing music.

I reverted to my teenage habits: lying on the floor, actively contemplating the meanings of song lyrics, taking five hours to eat breakfast and take a shower.

Also, I was running out of money.

When you run out of money in *The Sims* Build Mode, you leave Build Mode and start gameplay. And that's what I needed to do. I needed to download *The Sims*.

When I had a job, I had to pretend to be happy for at least part of the day. I wasn't beaming or anything. I wasn't some insane, smiling joker. But I had to act as if I were a relatively happy human being.

That science that suggests that the physical effort of smiling can trick one's brain into feeling happiness may be at least partially true.

But now I'm home almost all the time and, having exhausted many of my friends' capacities for compassion, I am able to devote full days to plotting petty revenge and going over my past failures ad nauseam.

I never smile because I never have to, which feels like a luxury meant only for rich people who don't have to work customer service.

And I don't feel happy, and I don't feel like I'm letting anyone down by not being happy, and I've never felt more like a millionaire or been further from one.

Untitled #11

I'M NOT IN THE RIGHT PLACE, EMOTIONALLY, TO SELL
MY ART FOR LESS THAN $5,000.

I dreamt I found my mom's diary and within it there was a section entitled THINGS I HATE ABOUT MY DAUGHTER. Below was a detailed list of every art project I had ever worked on, spanning back to my early childhood. There were hundreds of projects, many that I had forgotten about for years, each with detailed information about when I made it, what medium I was working in, and what I was inspired by at the time.

It was a great resource.

Untitled #12

YOU WEREN'T WRONG WHEN YOU SAID I WOULD GIVE
UP ON THE WORLD BEFORE IT GAVE UP ON ME.

I GUESS I JUST THOUGHT I WOULD BE THE FIRST TO
KNOW IF I HAD GIVEN UP ON THE WORLD.

The world is full of ridiculous scenarios that you have to accept and regard as meaningful. Water can turn into air before your eyes, for example. Evaporate.

Water that you might've been counting on could literally disappear from your life without a moment's notice, and everyone seems pretty much okay with that.

In fact, if you dared to comment on the unreliability of water, people would line up around the block just to get the chance to argue with you. That's how acceptable it is for water to just get up and decide to quit being water.

Doesn't it seem natural that people would behave the same way?

Like, couldn't I go from dating Mickey to not dating him to dating him to not dating him without anyone asking questions or asking me to explain anything?

Courtney seemed to be acting distant and weird while we prepared separate meals in the kitchen.

I hadn't seen her yet that day, and it was odd for her to ignore me.

I said, "Courtney, are you upset with me?"

She said, "Me?"

I said, "Yeah."

"Do I seem upset?"

"Yes."

"I do?"

She actually seemed less and less upset as our conversation progressed.

"Yes. Are you upset?"

She said, "I think I'm just sensitive to everyone. It's not you. It's not just you. I'm just sensitive."

"Are you sure?"

She said, "Yesterday you said something that made me sad, but I can't remember what it was. But it was just me being sensitive. It has nothing to do with you."

"What did I say to make you sad?"

"I can't remember. It's nothing."

I texted Courtney an anecdote about how someone at Starbucks spelled "sugar" wrong and that it made me think of her and her notoriously terrible spelling.

She texted back that she was charmed, which I took as evidence that she might not have been as charmed as she let on.

Considering the sequence of life, and, what the hell, considering scale and distribution and mass, and considering how all of those things are within a framework of, uh, and how they're organized within and according to each other, how things fit—I'm not just talking about biology, I'm talking about gravity, too—and the forces that are working together to express themselves as gravity, and how the forces of the universe come together, engage each other in these ways in a singular effort to push water through your faucet as you're washing your hands, considering all of this, um.

I arrived at Mickey's apartment crying and he asked me what was wrong. I threw myself onto the floor in front of him and he asked if *Project Runway* had made me cry.

I said that it had and he asked who was kicked off and I said, "Nobody, the judges let them all stay," and faintly pretended to weep, and Mickey told me I was crazy.

When people die, other people say that the dead people live in the hearts of the still-alive people, just like how the pixels of your email address live in other people's inboxes.

I said, "Do you know that game where you lie?"

Mickey said, "Yes. Life?"

"You tell two truths and a lie?"

"Yes. Everyday life. I know that one."

I said, "You tell two truths and a lie and the people try to guess what—"

"That's what every waking moment of my life is like."

"Okay. Well I guess you don't want to hear my story and would rather hear yourself tell the same joke five times in a row."

"No, tell me."

"No."

"Please tell me. I'm sorry."

"No."

I almost feel like I've gotten to a point where I don't feel lonely.

Or, I have a new understanding of the word "lonely" that doesn't imply sadness or a longing to connect, but refers to how good I am at hanging out with myself.

I wish I could say, "I wish I could make people love me," without seeming desperate.

I wish I could push Mickey as far from me as possible while still holding an invisible leash.

I would pull the leash so tightly that his love for me and my emotional manipulation would work symbiotically, like some kind of demented Escher tessellation.

I would demand that Mickey and I move in together and I would hang a print of an Escher tessellation in our living room and never tell him what it means to me. I'd tell him I'm just a fan of the artist. I'd become irrationally defensive if he asked too much about it.

My mom grew up not knowing her dad. My grandma refused to talk about him.

When my mom turned eighteen she was given her birth certificate, which identified her father. She recognized his name as the boyfriend of her best friend Laurie's mom.

In my mom's stories about her dad, she always alternated between calling him "my father" and "Laurie's mom's boyfriend."

They had lived in the same small town for eighteen years. They had barbequed together. They had shared Thanksgiving dinner together one year when my grandma was out of town. One time, he had told my mom not to bite her fingernails, and she had felt insulted and couldn't figure out why she cared what he thought.

She had never particularly liked him. She thought he was too loud and drank too much and always made comments about how beautiful other women were. She thought he was disrespectful to Laurie's mother.

She decided not to tell anyone that she knew the identity of her father. She had gone this long without one and it seemed overdramatic to try to have one now.

This story was told to me like a fairy tale as I grew up. It was the lore of my mother.

She didn't tell him that she knew he was her father, but my mom continued to see him periodically. She and Laurie only became closer after high school and they spent a lot of time with each other's families. They became pregnant at the same time, my mom with me, and Laurie with her son, Lucas (who I made out with once when I was fifteen when we were there for Christmas).

It occurred to her at some point that he must know she was his daughter. There weren't many secrets in their small town. It seemed impossible for him not to know. He, too, apparently, was actively making the decision not to talk to her about their relation to each other. Or, worse, she thought, he was leaving the responsibility of initiating the awkward conversation to my mom.

He died young of a heart attack. My mom and I flew back for the funeral and sat by Laurie and her mom. After the ceremony, my mom approached Laurie and Laurie's mom.

"I have something to say," my mom said. They looked at her tearfully. "He was my dad. I never told him."

"No, honey," Laurie's mom said. "I knew your dad." Laurie's mom described a man who, indeed, shared his name with the man who was now dead. A man who had moved to Wisconsin to live with his uncle and never returned.

My mom had spent ten years believing that someone was her dad when he wasn't. And now her real father was undead and possibly living in Wisconsin.

I called my cousin, Janine. My mom and I had been close with Janine at various points of my childhood and I thought they might still be in touch.

We talked for forty-five minutes about lots of things, from what we thought might be in our grandma's cioppino recipe to the mole on her back that had felt weird lately. My mom's name came up once, when Janine mentioned that her own hair currently looked like my mom's looked in 1998, after my mom had accidentally left bleach in it too long and had to cut it off to her ears. I inquired about the state of Janine's hair more than I ordinarily would have, feeling like we were talking about my mom even though we weren't, and then her baby started crying and we hung up.

I feel hesitant to do too much work to track down my mom because I don't know if I could respect someone who abandoned me without a word of explanation.

Then again, I don't know what respect has to do with anything.

Untitled # 13

NOSTRDAUMUS PREDICTED I WOULD FEEL SAD TODAY
AND EVERYDAY HEREAFTER.

There are lots of moments that people don't even notice are happening because they're preoccupied with some other aspect of your universe and because of the thousands of variations of people's eye movements and vocal fluctuations that one doesn't notice but which change everything about how one feels about oneself and the world. Because one really can't notice everything, it is impossible to pay attention to one thing without neglecting an infinite number of other things that are all happening simultaneously and all changing everything about how the future will look, seem, and feel like.

I'm trying this thing where I'm just letting life pass me by as it it's nothing.

"Your lovemaking strategies are formulaic," Mickey said. "I feel like I can tell what you have been reading based on the sequence of your movements."

I thought it was a romantic thing to say.

"What do you think I have been reading?" I said.

"I think you've been reading about stem cell research," he said.

I got up from the bed and found my shirt. I can't remember feeling insulted but I remember behaving in a way that could have been interpreted as such.

I've never had any strong opinions about stem cell research, so it couldn't have been that.

Idea for an art show:

I'll hire a woman to perform in a gallery space. She will be required to wander around the space, never talking, never making eye contact with anyone. I'll instruct everyone not to talk to her. The show will be called "BEST JUST LEAVE HER ALONE."

I will invite all her friends and loved ones to the show. I will invite her ex-boyfriends and people she was mean to in high school and the neighbor kid who she used to babysit who is now in college. I'll invite her ex-best friend who she hasn't talked to in eight years. I'll instruct all of these people not to talk to the performer under any circumstances.

I'll leave a comment book at the front of the gallery, and there will be a big sign over it that says PLEASE WRITE ANYTHING YOU WISH. But I will have informed everyone ahead of time that the only thing they're permitted to write is LOOKS LIKE YOU'RE DOING WELL and their own name.

I'm not ready to live in a world in which I feel obligated to admit I have an interest in performance art.

If I'm being gentle with myself, I will asterisk "performance art" and include a note about how performance includes popular and accessible means of artistic expression such as acting and singing.

But if I'm being hard on myself, I will imagine myself doing interpretive dance on a sidewalk as passersby pretend not to see me.

The awful feeling I get in my stomach when someone pretends not to see me doing interpretive dance on the sidewalk is what will drive me.

And when the stomach pain starts to become dull, I will go back to the sidewalk and interpret the stomach pain in a dance that I will consider my most important work to date, and the people of the sidewalk will pretend not to see me, and in that way the pain will feel fresh again.

I guess I have an interest in performance art.

I wish there was a time each day when everyone in the world had to stop what they were doing and make a list of a few things they liked about themselves. I bet it would make the rest of the day better.

I'd do it on my own but it seems like an embarrassing thing to do without an arbitrary, bureaucratic structure.

Arbitrary Bureaucratic Structure would be a good name for my imaginary performance art troupe.

I spent fifty-five dollars on my favorite kind of pens, even though I don't even have enough money for next month's rent, just to prove to the world or myself or some hypothetical otherworldly figure that I am absolutely terrible with money.

If I'm going down, I'm going down for the sake of art. If I'm going down, I'm going down for the sake of pens that would impress the fucking president of the art school that screwed me over. If I'm going down, I'm going to at least have the tools to draw something really fucking delicate and pretty.

My first boyfriend was named Ray. We were fifteen. Some-times, if my mom didn't feel like driving him home, he would be allowed to spend the night. We would share my single bed, spooning, our pants coming down as soon as all the lights in the house were off.

In this way, my mom chose when we had sex and when we did not have sex, except for twice when we had sex in Ray's parents' garage and once in the bathroom during an after school basketball game.

I cried the first time he told me he masturbated. I made him tell me what kinds of images he looked at while he did it. Was it pictures? Videos? Who was in these videos? Who was the unattainable object of his desire? Who was it whose image made his dick hard? Who was it that I would unfairly compare myself to for the rest of my life?

"Mostly Jennifer Lopez," Ray said.

Ray and I broke up after I drew a portrait of an attractive and charismatic male classmate in exchange for five dollars. The portrait had been passed around in class due to my rare artistic gift, and a friend of Ray's had seen it and told him.

"That's not cool," Ray had said. "You don't just do that for some other guy."

"It didn't mean anything," I said. But had it meant something? Had it not set off a chain reaction that I was proud of?

I guess I was starting to realize that art could be a tool.

I couldn't pay rent for October. Courtney's friend Slick offered to rent my room for the month, which I happily agreed to. So I am exiled to the couch.

(Courtney found the couch on the street a year ago. Right before she found it, I saw a homeless man with no pants sleeping on it. But I never said anything about it when she brought it home, and I secretly took pleasure in her not knowing, so now I can't really tell her that I don't want to sleep on the couch without explaining the homeless, pants-less guy and admitting that I withheld that information from her for my own amusement.)

All of my worldly possessions are stuffed into the hall closet, where I suspect they always thought they might end up.

I can't tell if I'm making the choice to be a total wreck in every avenue of my life or if there is some exterior force that's keeping me drugged and asleep in some Matrix-like existence (full disclosure: haven't seen the movie), and the drugs aren't set to the correct levels but no one in charge is paying attention, and this is all a horrible, hallucinatory nightmare that is happening to me through absolutely no fault of my own.

"Sometimes I think I should have studied architecture," said Mickey.

"Yep," I said. It was possibly the first time I had considered the word "architecture" in five years. I wondered briefly what the word "architecture" had been up to since the last time I had heard it.

"What do you mean, 'yep'?" he said.

I wish I were more interested in architecture. I think highly of people who have an interest in the way a building works. I don't know quite how to put this, because I have no background or interest in architecture, but something about it seems cerebral. The consideration of how people might move in and out of a structure, how they might feel inside of it, and what it would look like from a distance seem like they should be pretty far at the top of one of those pyramids that explain how the needs of humans are organized—where food and shelter are at the bottom, art and love are higher, spirituality is somewhere above that maybe—and I think architecture would be at the top, the pinnacle of luxurious creative output.

"You've always shown an interest in architecture," I said.

"I don't know what I ever said to make you feel that way," he said.

I feel preemptively defensive about my worldview, as if I know it will be an unpopular choice amongst my peers, as if I am choosing an unpopular worldview on purpose to feel differentiated and disconnected, and my preemptive defense toward them proves that I care what they think and want to feel prepared for their criticism, as if my confidence and preparedness on the subject could prove to them how right I am and how wrong they are, and as if having my defenses up when they undoubtedly criticize me will protect me from the pain their disagreement will cause me, which I have preemptively decided I don't care about, but which definitively proves that I do.

Untitled #14

I DON'T KNOW IF I'VE EVER BEEN REALLY LOVED BY A
HAND THAT'S TOUCHED ME.

My favorite part of life is that it feels like a long dramatic interpretation of "Push" by Matchbox 20.

I asked Slick if he had an Instagram account and he said, "Yes!" so aggressively and condescendingly that you would've thought I had asked if he was born on Earth, which got me thinking about Kate Winslet, because the implication that there was some other planet to be born on got me thinking about the moon, which seemed, for some reason, like the most likely non-Earth place a person could be born (I guess my imagination is somewhat limited), and I started thinking about man landing there in the fifties or whatever, and the conspiracy theories around that, which obviously made me start thinking of R.E.M.'s song "Man on the Moon" and the film of the same name which was about the life of Andy Kaufman and not really the moon at all, from what I can remember. The title must have been some kind of metaphor, and that led to thinking about Jim Carrey's career, specifically his role in *Eternal Sunshine of the Spotless Mind*, which I always think of as his best performance, and which also starred Kate Winslet.

But Kate Winslet doesn't seem to have an Instagram account, so this has failed to come full circle, and proves that life is an exercise in futility.

Of course I want to believe that the moon, inexplicably visible in the sunny sky, has a relationship with the sun that is difficult or impossible for us humans to comprehend, and that the decisions they (the sun and moon) make together are responsible for my sudden, inexplicable changes in mood on days when I otherwise feel in control of my body. I'd love for my blood and cells to be communicating with the sky in a language designed to trick me into believing that I am a cognizant, living creature who is checking her own pulse at night after watching so many clips of *What Not To Wear* on YouTube that I feel it may have killed me.

What is more annoying than a semi-homeless, semi-employed, pretty hungry (but not technically starving) self-identified artist who hasn't had a show since graduating from art school five years ago and is asking into an abyss what the abyss considers more annoying than some other particular thing?

Courtney said, "What do you want to do for Halloween?"

I said, "I'm not going to do anything. I don't like dressing up and I don't care about Halloween, and every year on Halloween I'm expected to have fun and I never do and I don't care." She said, "That Jono guy invited me to a party. I think he invited everyone."

I said, "Oh, that guy. I used to be in love with him."

She said, "Really? That's surprising. Who else have you been in love with?"

I sighed, and in an overly condescending tone I said, "It's difficult to remember, Courtney."

When I was fired in July, I had enough money to get through September.

The phrase "figure it out" figured into my life a lot at that point, as if my life were an equation that simply required some concentration and the correct sequence of formulas.

In August, I changed the phrase to "things will work out," trying to take the pressure off of myself to "figure out" anything. My inherent lack of skills, qualifications, or job-related experience was becoming a real issue.

Near the end of September, I found a job organizing a nutritionist's filing cabinet and responding to her emails ten hours a week for minimum wage, with a promised two-dollar raise after six weeks.

Her name is Melinda. She doesn't seem to like me.

I can see the bones poking out of Melinda's skull. The way she holds her head makes it look intentional, like she thinks head bones are naturally sexy.

She has a big old house that smells like vitamins, and I work in the basement where she keeps her files and computer as well as her collection of insect corpses, mounted and framed and stacked along the walls.

"I'm directing a health retreat next weekend and there are a couple empty spaces, if you'd like to go." Melinda said.

"Oh, cool," I said. "Where is it?"

"It's at The Harbor Spa Center. I could give you fifteen percent off."

"Oh, okay. I probably won't be able to."

Melinda asked me to come in an extra day to transcribe some notes from her nutritionist's retreat into a word processor.

"I'm sure you'll be tempted to read the notes and try to glean data that you can use in your life," she said. "But just remember that not only is that unethical and technically information theft, but also that those nutrition profiles are based on an individual's particular needs, and you could end up really hurting yourself if you follow a diet created for someone else."

"Okay," I said. "I'm actually pretty good at reading without retaining information."

"Well, I should hope so."

I read the documents slowly and carefully as I transcribed them, trying to retain information just to spite Melinda.

I thought, *I should really become a nutritionist.*

I thought, *I mean it this time.*

Sometimes I fantasized about having an affair with Melinda's ex-husband, Paul, who she was still close with and who came over to make repairs at her house on a regular basis.

If there was a squeaky doorknob, paint chipping off a corner, or a mysterious cat that wouldn't leave the yard, Paul would arrive, check his phone a million times, and then leisurely attend to the issue at hand.

He had a slight lisp and frequently used my name when speaking or referring to me.

It would be perfect. Our entire relationship would consist of giving each other meaningful looks at Melinda's house when we thought she wasn't looking.

Melinda would get suspicious and jealous and fire me for some convoluted, unrelated, weirdly specific reason (the disruptive way I moved around the house), and then I wouldn't have to work there anymore, and Paul would feel like he had to take care of me out of some masculine duty.

I would borrow money from him, buy myself a professional wardrobe, and get a respectable, art-related job in an industry that inspired and respected me.

I would have to leave him to pursue my career. He wouldn't ask me any questions about my decision when I left.

Years later, I would describe the time around my relationship with Paul as my "troubled years," and people would encourage me to make work about it.

I'd make a whole series dedicated to his lisp and then refuse to talk about him for years.

Those would be my "mysterious years."

Paul called for Melinda while she was out running errands.

"Do you want me to take a message?" I said.

"That's okay, I'll call back later."

"Okay, well Melinda should be back in an hour."

"I'll probably just try her cell phone."

"Okay, that works, too."

"Yeah, I probably should have tried the cell phone first so I didn't distract you."

"No, it's no problem."

"So can you tell Melinda I called?"

"Yeah, of course."

"Or I can just mention I called the office before I tried her cell phone."

"That works, too."

"Alright, thank you, bye."

"No problem at all."

"Bye."

"Bye."

Mickey sent me a text that said he was craving tiramisu, so I went to the bakery and bought a slice for us as a surprise.

We ate a big dinner together and afterward I wasn't in the mood for tiramisu, but I didn't want it to get soggy so I decided to serve it.

"Time for dessert," I said. Mickey made a confused facial expression, possibly suggesting that I was lying and/or fucking with him about it being time for dessert. I went to the fridge and pulled out the box, which had obviously been opened.

"You opened the box," I said.

"What is it?" he said.

"You looked at it," I said.

"So what?" he said. "I talked about it earlier, so it's not that big of a surprise."

I had a strong urge to throw the tiramisu into the trash. Instead I handed it to Mickey and walked out of the apartment.

I think there can't be anything more shameful and humiliating than being rejected by your own mom, so, by comparison, standing in the dark, empty street silently crying about tiramisu that had been seen before it was served felt calm and rational.

I started brainstorming a TV pilot based on my relationship with Mickey: two people in love, traveling the world, making public art projects and learning about each other and growing together through our work. In each episode, we would show up in a town, meet the locals, go to a few iconic places, get a general sense of what the town was about and who lived there, and let that, along with our own artistic identities and interests, help inform the content of our art project in the town. At the end of each episode, we would say what we learned about ourselves, each other, the town we were in, the artistic implications of our experience, the extent of our love, etc.

Mickey interrupted my fantasy. "So do you want to build the raised beds for your garden tomorrow? Or did you have other plans?"

I was kind of wrapped up in the television show I was imagining so I said, "I don't know. Can we talk about it tomorrow?" Maybe during some of the episodes, we would fight or disagree, and the people we met would help bring us back together and show us what was really important.

"Okay. Or I could build the frames by myself and you could do the chicken wire and burlap? I just feel like if we don't do it tomorrow you won't be able to plant your seeds in time. I mean, we're already kind of getting a late start. Do you have an opinion, or . . . ?"

By this point it felt like we were going through the motions of a pre-determined conversation. It seemed like there was literally nothing I could say except, "Can we talk about it tomorrow?"

"Well, yeah. I mean, I don't see why. It's not like you're doing anything. You're just sitting there."

"I would prefer to talk about it tomorrow. I don't feel like talking about it right now."

"Well, I do."

"Well, I don't."

I was beginning to lose track of some of the details of the TV pilot.

Mickey said, "What, am I being annoying to you?" which was like the Bermuda Triangle of our arguments together, the point of no return. We would start talking about the fight, and for the rest of the conversation we would each try to dig ourselves out of the hole that is a meta-analysis of an in-session argument while still maintaining the tone of and reasons for the original argument, both of us refusing to admit that we have no idea that we're losing sight of what the argument is about because we're both determined to win.

I said, "Yes." And with that we left the world of concrete reality to talk about tones of voices, intent, implied intent, and mood, all of which could never be verified, and could therefore be conveniently misrepresented to serve a point.

And Mickey said, "You're the one who wants the raised beds." "I just wish you would respect the fact that I don't want to talk about something the second you want to talk about it."

"Well, I don't know. How am I supposed to know how serious you're being?"

"You should trust that I'm being honest when I'm telling you exactly what I want."

"Okay, well I didn't know."

I said, "Okay," and didn't look at him and still felt definitively mad for a reason that seemed to be incoherent, extremely vague, and semi-violent.

Mickey said, "Look, let's not fight. I was just trying to engage with you."

I said, "Can you give me a butt massage now?" as some kind of peacemaking opportunity for Mickey to perform (and in reference to some minor butt muscle pain I had been experiencing, not just a random request).

My food came twenty minutes after Mickey's, and in that twenty minutes I had grown so hungry and frustrated that when my food arrived I literally lost my vision (which has to be what people mean when they say "blind rage"), and for the couple of seconds in which I experienced this blind rage, I picked up my wasabi ball with my chopsticks and hurled it violently into the wall next to our table.

I logged onto my fake Facebook account and saw that my mom had posted the music video for a White Stripes song I had introduced her to ten years ago that she told me at the time she didn't think was very interesting. I sent her a message from the fake account, asking how she was doing and why she hadn't responded to any of my texts and why she blocked me on Facebook. Later, I saw that the message was marked as read. She hadn't responded but she hadn't blocked my fake Facebook profile, either.

Sometimes I will put a not-very-sad song on and sing it while practicing to cry and stop crying on command. Sometimes I videotape myself doing this. At first I thought it was art, but now I think maybe it's something else.

I want to draw a portrait that combines facial features in such a way that it makes everyone in my life think it is a portrait of them.

I want them to look at the portrait, to try to understand my reasons for drawing them, conjuring memories of us or our time together that they think might have inspired me.

I want them to reconsider everything they thought they knew about our relationship.

I want them to look deeply into the eyes they think are a rendering of their own eyes, seeing nothing but reflections of everything they've ever done or said to me that might have caused me to make such a portrait of them.

I want them to try to imagine how it must feel to be me when I think of them, and feel embarrassed by how much love is looking back at them.

I want them to feel important and powerful for being the subject of my portrait, and then I want them to feel embarrassed and ashamed of themselves for feeling proud of causing the pain required to draw such a portrait, the pain being implied by the title of the piece, which would be SOURCE OF THE ARTIST'S PAIN.

Mickey and I went on a hike to look for mushrooms at Huckleberry Preserve. Well, not really looking. Our friend warned us there would not be any mushrooms there, but we hadn't asked about mushrooms.

We went to Huckleberry Preserve anyway, not caring one way or the other about whether there would be mushrooms.

We didn't see any mushrooms.

It wasn't a very close friend.

I was wrapped in a blanket with my face pressed into the corner of the couch when Courtney and Slick came home.

They didn't say anything or look at me to see whether or not my eyes were open. They just silently walked through the hallway into their respective bedrooms and shut their doors.

I wondered how accurately either one of them could describe my appearance. How close a police sketch artist could get to my physicality based only on the descriptive words of the people I lived with.

I wondered if Slick thought I was doing him a favor by renting him my room, or if he thought he was doing me a favor by renting my room.

I wondered if Courtney was in love with Slick, or if I was in love with Slick, or if either of us could know if we were in love with him or if we were both too emotionally stunted to understand our own feelings. I wondered if Slick was in love with either of us, or anyone, or had ever felt a feeling he would ever have described as love at any point in his life, or if it was any of my business to wonder about things like that, and if it wasn't my business, then who could possibly stop me.

I realized I had started masturbating and stopped myself, then started again while imagining myself straddling Slick on the couch. In my fantasy Courtney came home, saw us naked together on the couch but pretended not to see us, then snuck into her room and wept, realizing for the first time that she was in love with Slick. We could hear her crying from the living room.

"Don't stop," I imagined saying to Slick, who was just discovering in this moment that he, too, was in love with Courtney.

He didn't stop, and I got off while thinking about keeping two people in love away from each other.

I started fantasizing about an undiscovered color that was the perfect mixture of red and blue before realizing that it already exists and it's purple.

Some Ideas:

An art piece where I sing "You Ain't Seen Nothing Yet" with such a severe stutter that it takes all year.

A performance art piece where I fall asleep reading *Lord of the Flies* and when I wake up everyone takes me super seriously.

An art film that documents my life following the publication of my collected works art book with Taschen, after which I get a ton of artistic exposure and lots of "cool connections" but it doesn't help me get a job, and I have to request that the local library obtains a copy of my Taschen book so I can see it because I can't afford to buy one and I had my artist copies sent to my mom's old address because I'm also homeless.

A performance art piece where I vocally berate the pads of my own fingertips in public until a stranger approaches and tells me that the pads of my fingertips are lovely and uniquely mine and that I should cherish them.

A fiber arts project where I meticulously embroider all my darkest thoughts onto large pieces of fabric, and then cut the pieces into small pieces and mix them up and sew them together to make a quilt, which I then spend the rest of my life actively treasuring.

"Are you going to have enough money to pay for your room in November?" Courtney said.

"Hmmmmmmmmmmmmmmmm," I said.

"Because Slick said he would be interested in staying another month."

"Oh, yeah. Then that's perfect," I said.

"Okay. But you're still going to sleep on the couch?"

"Where would you have me sleep?"

"It's just that I'd kind of like to have a living room again."

"Right."

"Well, it's not a big deal if it's only another month," she said.

"True," I said.

I wrote a craigslist ad for a new roommate. I described what I wanted in a roommate: "definitely not an artist . . . someone who describes their personal style as 'vintage Hot Topic,' I'm talking zippers, red plaid, studded belts, a few more zippers . . . " and then described Courtney's bedroom, the square footage of the living room, and how the refrigerator was organized. I set up a new email account to collect responses. I never logged into the email account, though, so I don't know if anyone ever replied.

One metaphysical experience from today:

Slick turned the lights on when he got in at 4:00 a.m., and I guess he didn't realize or care that I was sleeping on the couch because he left the lights on when he left the living room, and then closed the door to the bedroom that used to be mine.

I'm a fan of Courtney's paintings, especially her "Hair" series. She is technically talented and has some good ideas, and I do believe she deserves the success she has achieved.

Her website is nice.

I know how diligent and disciplined she is, and I know that she has had to overcome many hurdles, such as the death of her little sister (though I'm not sure that a list of horrible experiences is an indicator of talent or deservedness).

Perhaps it's jealousy, but it feels more complicated than that. My work suffers an inferior rate of commercial acceptance because I am more self-critical and quick to abandon my work. The difference between Courtney and I, artistically, is her superior level of follow-through and confidence. She shows in the galleries I want to show in because she is able to put off unproductive critical thought until she has completed the piece. Where Courtney would finish a piece regardless of her shifting intentions or interest in the subject matter, I abandon my work and move onto a new project. The failure is what drives me to continue.

Failing at art is what moves me.

"These pieces are about beauty ideals," Courtney said. "How we use hair and clothing to wordlessly portray our deeper selves to others. Hair is symbolic of a person's unending need to be understood."

"Oh," I said. "I thought they were about how strange and animalistic it is that people are so into hair when hair is just oil and protein and dead cells."

"That's an interesting interpretation."

Symbolism is a way of talking about something without addressing it explicitly, leaving interpretation to the viewer, who can project their own interests and feelings onto the art, thereby making the art more powerful.

Not sure what the difference between symbolism and sarcasm is.

Untitled #15

I DON'T LIKE ART UNLESS THE ARTIST HAS ADMITTED
FAILURE.

I DON'T LIKE ARTISTS UNLESS THEY HATE THEMSELVES.

ALSO, I HATE MURALS.

"I can't take this seriously," Courtney said. "I feel like you're making fun of the part of the art world that you don't want anything to do with anyway. What's the point?"

"Is sarcasm not a valid artistic subject?"

"Sarcasm is fine, I guess. I just think it's a cop out. Why don't you try to access something true and deep inside yourself, instead of covering it up with falseness and sarcasm?"

"What if I'm just deeply, relentlessly, authentically sarcastic?"
"If you are then there's something even deeper that's causing you to be that way. Maybe fear of rejection? A desire for approval and love? I would be interested in seeing work exploring that."

"What if under the sarcasm were layers and layers of more sarcasm, and beneath all those layers is nothing but a tiny little nugget of brown poop? Would you be interested in seeing work exploring that?"

"Poop?" Courtney said.

"Poop," I said.

Just one example of why I'm right:

Love is an evolutionary adaptation that humans developed to better survive in numbers, allowing them to simultaneously support and benefit from their "loved ones."

This fact is usually ignored in artistic portrayals of love, instead appealing to our superficial understanding of it—the feeling of having it or losing it, how it looks on our faces, how it affects our behavior, how symbols of it can be found in anything if we look hard enough.

What if I insisted that art "simply" about love was a shallow cop out? That I was only interested in art about love if it called attention to these deeper evolutionary urges?

But I didn't pose these questions to Courtney, because it's hard to argue against love and easy to disregard sarcasm as boring and immature.

Maybe Courtney is projecting her fear of not knowing herself onto me by telling me I am the one who doesn't understand myself.

Maybe sarcasm is not a mask to hide my true self from the world, but colored glasses that help me appreciate its beauty.

Courtney showed a painting in a group show last year, and someone who attended the show invited her to participate in a second group show, and then someone who attended the opening of that show and who was friends with the curator interviewed Courtney for some local arts magazine, and then a gallery owner saw the article and contacted Courtney and asked her if she wanted a solo show in his gallery, so eight months later Courtney showed eighteen new pieces in the gallery and sold four pieces opening night, and last night she received an email from someone at *Juxtapoz Magazine* asking if she would be interviewed for a feature and a second email inviting her to do another solo show next year.

Which is all so great.

There's no other word for it, despite my great efforts to come up with another word for it.

"I need to talk to you," I said.

Mickey said, "I can't talk. Why should I talk to you?"

"Because you love me."

"I don't think you love me."

I came home from seventh grade one day and my mom and her boyfriend, David, were talking quietly in the living room. I could tell my mom was upset and had been crying. I passed them without saying anything and tried to eavesdrop from my bedroom. I wasn't particularly interested in their relationship, but I had never seen them speak so quietly to each other. Maybe there had been a death.

My mom came into my bedroom after David left. I was painting Limp Bizkit lyrics onto the bottoms of my shoes.

"I broke up with David," she said.

"Oh," I said. "I was hoping someone died."

"I didn't like who I was becoming around him."

"Who were you becoming?"

"I realized I was just laughing at things I didn't think were funny. I was suggesting bars I didn't like. Pretending I liked flavored coffee creamers."

"Oh."

"If you can't be yourself around someone, they're not worth any of your time."

I love that old saying that goes, "What if our entire universe exists inside the dripping eye booger dispatched from some creature infinitely bigger than anything any human has ever tried to imagine?"

I like to think of my actions as being necessary to the success of this eye booger, that my actions are innate and required of me in order to support our universe's existence even though I am only a tiny, meaningless, temporary mechanism in this all-encompassing, ever-crusting eye booger, and probably not even a very big eye booger compared to all the other eye boogers this creature has had or will have, not to mention the other, probably larger creatures with probably larger eye boogers.

I like to think that my actions and emotions are not only not trivial and lame and kind of embarrassing, but that they're somehow vital to the success of not only our little electron universe, but also to the eye booger that supports our universe. That the items and experiences that have influenced my emotions—the books I've read, the art I've seen, the art I've made, television, the Internet I've browsed, the course names of the classes I took in college, and the number of utensils in my kitchen—are all part of the mechanism that gets me to feel what I need to feel to get me to do what is required of me so that I may support the system, our universe, before it, our precious eye booger, inevitably detaches from our charitable host and we (the eye booger, the many universes that make it up, our little planet within it, me, Mickey, Alexei, Courtney, Jason, Cameron Diaz, the Nancy Drew books I pretended to read for school credit, the miscarriage I once dreamt about, everyone's individual experience with *Grand Theft Auto*, an anonymous fart I once heard emitted at a camp fire, the women who play sister wives on *Big Love*, all the items I've ever favorited on Etsy, etc.) will combine in death and be forgotten together, all as equals.

Mickey said, "I was bored at work today so I started listening to an Alan Watts audio book and I asked myself how I came to be doing that in that moment, and it was because I heard about it on the Shroomery website, and I asked myself why I was on the Shroomery website and it was because I heard about it on the mushroom camping trip we went on last spring, and I asked myself why I went on that camping trip and it was because Caleb invited us, and I asked myself why I knew Caleb and it was because Jason introduced us to them, and I asked myself why I know Jason and it was because I know you."

I said, "It's not my fault you hate your fucking job."

Mickey said, "I'm saying that you're the source of a lot of good things in my life."

"Oh. That's sort of sweet."

When I was fourteen, my mom's boyfriend was a man named Rick who asked me to call him "sir." As in, like, "Would you be so kind as to give me a ride to Wal-Mart in your rusty, disgusting pickup truck, sir, so I might buy some feminine hygiene products before the commencement of my period?" Or, "Kind sir, can you please put your boots back on, because the smell of your feet is giving me something of a migraine. Alternately, you could nap somewhere other than our living room floor."

My mom once drunkenly confided in me that she had secretly hoped, while pregnant, that I would turn out to have
special needs. She thought my special needs could be the
motivation she needed to overcome her selfish inclinations,
become a better person, and learn to love things that are out
of one's control. She had heard some inspirational stories
from mothers who overcame such obstacles. Obstacles they
never expected to have to deal with but obstacles that ended up enriching their lives, healing wounds they never knew
were there.

A missing limb, I suppose. An extra chromosome. A devas-
tating inability to connect with humans and a well guarded
secret talent that presented itself late in my childhood.

But I was healthy and I developed normally. I loved to play
like a monkey in the trees and color quietly in my room and
help smaller children at the park. My independence came
between us before I was old enough to understand what the
word "independence" meant.

In third grade I asked for help with some division homework I
found difficult and my mom yelled at me for faking stupidity.
I was playing mind games, I was told, and using my intelligence to manipulate her.

I know this because my mom has cited it several times over
the years as an example of my habit of patronizing her, asking for her help purely to make her feel useful, as though I
thought myself to be the only source of affirmation she had
in this world. As if I pitied her uselessness. As if the fact that

addition and subtraction and multiplication were easy meant that division couldn't be hard.

"You've always been good at math," she had said, looking me hard in the eyes.

It was memorable to me, too. I remember realizing that I had some strange kind of power over my mom, but that she seemed to be unconsciously using that power against herself. Making us both powerless to it.

The negative space I imagine surrounding my body is a sort of comfort to me on lonely days. It surrounds me wherever I go, enveloping my body like a custom mattress, sometimes seeming to prevent movement, crushing me, reforming my body. But its existence depends on my body being there to appear around and my self-conscious brain perpetually trying to find a distraction from itself, and in this sense it is dependent on me in the most basic way, truly and totally reliant on my attention to it.

I was mad because Mickey didn't answer his phone any of the thirty times I'd called him the night before. He'd claimed he'd left his phone in his car, but that only proved he hadn't considered calling or texting me at all the entire night, while I'd spent the night thinking about how much I wanted to talk to him. I was suddenly aware of the discrepancy in our mutual interest in each other; he had the upper hand. I had no choice but to play defense and/or act psycho.

I hadn't been able to work on my drawings because I was too mad at him and also angry with myself for allowing his behavior to control my artistic output. And I was mad that he didn't want to watch *I Heart Huckabees* with me like I thought he had implied he wanted to do the night before when I said I liked the movie and he said he had never seen it. I said, "Oh, you should definitely see it, it's really good," and he said, "Cool, I will," and I said, "I own a copy," and he said, "Let's watch it together soon," which in retrospect didn't necessarily mean we would watch it the next night, but that was one hole I could not dig myself out of.

When I finally saw him, I was still upset about the same stuff but I wanted him to believe that I was upset about how he never wanted to take me on a real date or made a big effort to prepare dinner for me. He apologized and said he would cook dinner for me, but I thought that wasn't a very good answer and I told him he needed to try harder to impress me.

"I don't know how to impress you," he said.

"No," I said. "You don't."

"Fine," he said. "Maybe I should leave."

And I said, "Fine."

We stood there alternating between looking at each other and looking at the furniture in my apartment. I understood that we were having some kind of moment.

I was firm in my decision not to be the first person to say something.

Mickey was standing by the door, which I initially recognized to be symbolic of his position in my life.

But then I couldn't believe I was thinking something so stupid.

Today was a day I had to hurl my body into the places I knew it needed to go. "To survive," I told it, "you must shower." I gathered all my physical energy, crossed my eyes slightly to blur my vision, and leapt up from the bed, imagining my body as a skillfully shot arrow, aiming for the bathroom. Once there, I reasoned that it would be okay to lie in the tub instead of standing, and I let the water spray over me while I rested my eyes. I held a bar of soap up to the showerhead, allowing myself to believe that the soapy water falling in my general direction was somehow cleaning my body. I scraped a piece of mold off the shower curtain with my fingernail for thirty minutes and then got out of the shower without having accomplished much of anything.

Afterward, I stared at myself in the mirror trying to think of something to think about myself.

"Cry," I said. "If you're so sad, why don't you cry."

Based on how easily people who once loved me seem to be able to cut me off, and based on how easy it is for me to accept it, I can only assume that love is a temporary indulgence, never to be trusted. Love can only last when one doesn't truly care that/if it exists at all.

Honestly, there wouldn't really be a point to contacting Mickey, other than force of habit.

Though he is good at it, he doesn't owe it to me to make me feel better.

I had to delete his number from my phone. I could imagine too many moments in which I might think it was a good idea to text or call him.

I slept in my mom's bed at any opportunity until my teens. When she would break up with a boyfriend, the left side of her bed would be unoccupied, and we both understood it was my spot to sleep.

It felt like the left side of the bed had always been mine, and that my mom and I had both endured a man sleeping in it for complicated reasons.

I used to think that my mom and I were close during my childhood. But looking back, I can see that our closeness was mostly made up of telling each other that we were close, as if that's all it took.

"You can tell me anything," my mom would sometimes say. "I would never judge you." But when had I ever confided in her?

"You're the only person who has ever been there for me," I remember saying. It was a cliché I had heard that I assumed applied to my life, too.

But I didn't know why she did the things she did, and she didn't have much curiosity about the things I did, either. I didn't try to understand her at all, I merely accepted her and thought about other things. We were mostly nice to each other, but how could I have ever thought that was closeness?

Perhaps the left side of the bed was not my side of the bed but just an unoccupied side of the bed that my mom didn't care much about.

I remember I was upset about something a couple years ago.

It's not that I can't remember what I was upset about, it's that I didn't know what I was upset about at the time.

I tried to think of some upsetting things, hoping something would stand out as the trigger of my depressive mood, but nothing in particular stood out.

Maybe I wanted to be upset. Or maybe there was something troubling deep within me that was trying to make itself known. Like a small bruise that's so unnoticeable that you keep pressing it to make sure it's there, which only makes it larger and more noticeable.

Whatever it was, I decided to call my mom.

"Do you want to call me back when you're finished crying?" my mom said.

"No," I said. "I'll stop."

"Well, it doesn't sound like you're stopping."

I have tried to make myself feel larger by attaching myself to other people, but all the people moved away from me smoothly and quietly as if they didn't notice my attachment to them at all. Now the people are so far away that they look tiny, and I feel larger and more important by comparison.

Maybe that was my plan all along.

Untitled # 16

ART THAT REFERS TO ITSELF AS "ART" IS LOWBROW, BUT CALLING THAT SAME ART "SEMINAL" AND EATING CHEESE AROUND IT MAKES IT HIGHBROW, BUT ACKNOWLEDGING THE CHEESE IS LOWBROW, BUT CASUALLY EXPECTING CHEESE IS HIGHBROW, BUT FINDING AND PURCHASING THE SAME CHEESE FROM THE GROCERY STORE AT A LATER DATE FOR PRIVATE CONSUMPTION IS LOWBROW, BUT BUYING SOME OTHER CHEESE IS HIGHBROW, BUT SERVING IT TO ANYONE WHO DOESN'T CONSIDER THEMSELVES AN ARTIST IS LOWBROW, BUT SO IS CONSIDERING ONESELF AN ARTIST.

I came home drunk one night.

I was worried I would yell at Courtney, so I tried to concentrate on the words, "Don't yell at Courtney," which started to lose meaning through internal repetition.

It didn't matter, though, because nobody was home.

I stood in Slick's room with the light off in case Slick came home and saw his light on from outside. Light came into the room from the kitchen, so I could still see.

The room had remained pretty much the same since I had lived in it. My mattress was still pushed into the same corner. My heavy wood desk still stood opposite the bed, but was now empty of the piles of paper and old jam jars filled with paint that I usually kept there. The clean surface made the desk look less "old desk" and more "vintage desk."

In place of my art supplies, there was a neat stack of unopened mail.

"Mail art," I thought drunkenly.

It occurred to me that Courtney and I had not discussed whether Slick would be moving out or renting my room the next month.

I could pay for rent if I needed to, but I'd be left with basically no money, and it seemed unlikely that I could get rent money together in time for the next month.

Maybe it would never be my room again.

"How is your mom?" Courtney asked. She was painting her fingernails. I was watching a documentary on my laptop about how aliens may have created mankind.

"I haven't talked to my mom in, like, a year," I said.

"Why not?" Courtney said.

I had been waiting for Courtney to ask me about my mom. I had imagined it and hoped for it and wondered why she hadn't asked yet. I had simulated conversations alone in my bedroom, or on the couch once I had no bedroom, in which Courtney counseled me and listed multiple reasons why my mom may have stopped talking to me, each of them conceivable, each of them reasonable, each of them things I hadn't thought of yet and that made me feel better about the situation.

I hate initiating my own emotionally loaded conversations, but I didn't want to lose the opportunity to talk about the only thing I actually wanted to talk about.

I turned the volume down on the alien documentary by a few notches.

"I don't know," I said. "She won't respond to anything."

"What happened?"

"I don't know."

"Okay," she said.

"*I don't know why*," I said, emphasizing each word to impress upon Courtney the importance of what I was saying.

"I called her but she won't answer. And then I lost her number when I broke my phone a few months ago. She moved and I don't know how to contact her. She blocked me on Facebook."

"Oh my god," Courtney said. "That's crazy. What are you going to do?"

"What can I do? What would you do?"

Courtney gestured to my hands, indicating that she wanted to paint my nails. I extended my fingers in front of her and she began painting them neon blue.

"Do you know someone who might have her number?" she asked.

"I guess."

I went to San Francisco to hang out with Logan.

I met Logan in a figure drawing class a few years before. We had spoken a couple of times in class and saw each other at parties sometimes, but it always seemed like we weren't that interested in each other. Like, on any level. Like, it seemed really boring and tedious to talk to each other, even if we were talking about something that interested us both. I felt like I'd rather talk to almost anyone else, even someone I hated, because Logan was just so unsurprising and lacked any sort of mystery or charisma.

Logan, for his part, seemed to make equal effort to never talk to me.

So it was odd that Logan texted and asked me to hang out. And it surprised me when I accepted the invitation.

But I should probably point out that Logan is very attractive.

We went to a punk show. Logan paid for forties of malt liquor that we wrapped in paper bags and brought into the show. We stood near the stage for the duration of the show, not speaking even during the intervals between songs. The music was almost as boring as the company.

After the show Logan bought us Coors tallboys and we drank them in an alley in the Mission.

"I'm reading a book about human evolution," Logan said.

"Oh, cool," I said.

"But it, like, starts with humans and then describes our nearest ancestor, and then the nearest ancestor after that, and all the other species that evolved from each species."

"Oh, is it *Ancestor's Tale?*"

"Yeah."

"Yeah, that book is cool."

"Really cool."

"Yeah, it's cool to see how exactly we are related to whales or mold or bobcats."

"Yep."

It was amazing how unenthusiastic we could be while agreeing that something was really cool.

We took BART back to my house. I assumed he would drop me off and leave, but he wanted to come in and hang out more. We drank from a flask of whiskey he had in his backpack.

I kissed him so we wouldn't feel awkward about not talking. "Should we go to your bedroom?" he said.

"I'm sleeping on the couch while our friend is staying with us."

"Oh," he said. "Should we go to my apartment?"

"Sure."

We walked a mile and a half to Logan's apartment, passing the flask back and forth on the way. It was almost 3:00 a.m. when we arrived at his place. I tiptoed into his dark apartment so that we wouldn't wake his roommates, but he turned the lights on and it turned out he lived in a studio apartment by himself.

We kissed on his unmade bed, took off our pants, then decided we were too drunk to go any further and passed out on opposite sides of the bed.

In the morning, Logan made us coffee, pancakes, bacon, and scrambled eggs, surprising me yet again with the amount of effort he took to make breakfast (it took an hour) while seemingly completely uninterested in anything I said. We ate on his tiny, sunny patio.

"Do you want to take a walk?" he said when we were done eating.

"I should go," I said.

"Okay, I'll call you later," he said.

I found forty dollars on the street and decided to "treat my-self" to buying toilet paper for the apartment, because I hadn't purchased household items for several months and it's been taxing on my interpersonal leverage.

I bought the softest, fluffiest toilet paper to let my roommates know that I think they deserve the best.

Logan texted, "Whatsup?"

Three hours later I replied, "Not much."

Three days later he texted, "Consciousness is really hard to imagine."

The next day, "Sorry, was stoned."

Eight days after that he texted, "Four weeks until knee surgery."

Two minutes later he texted, "Ignore that. Wrong person."

I posted a photo of Mickey and me on my Facebook profile to make people wonder if we were back together.

Judy, a former classmate from art school, was promoting a solo show she was having in our city, and I was invited via a comment under the photo.

"Aw, miss you 2! You shld come to my show next thurs," she wrote. She also pasted a link to the gallery's website.

"OMG Def," I wrote.

Nobody else commented, probably because no one wanted to participate in a comment thread that had been hijacked by some random girl's art show.

Weeks later, I wrote a comment under the same photograph, "Sorry I didn't come to your show :(t'was so busy," as if it were an appropriate place to have a conversation about her art show opening or my availability to attend it, as if this pixilated representation of the happy relationship that I failed to hold onto but that was still present in this photograph had anything to do with my former classmate's inflated ego or budding art career.

One time, early in our relationship, I came home from work and found Mickey on my bed. He had been in my apartment all day, using my plumbing, flipping through my books.

"I wanted to hang out with your stuff," he said. It was the sweetest thing he had said to me up until that point.

Sometimes I remember so clearly the feeling of being in that room looking at Mickey, trying to come up with a way to respond.

I guess I felt proud that someone was making an attempt to understand me.

In retrospect, I can see that my belongings are no more "me" than the individual pixels that make up my email address on my mom's computer screen at the top of an email I sent her a year ago.

I once told Mickey, "I love you because you make me feel like I don't need to say it."

This was a mistake, not only because that wasn't at all why I loved him, but also because it underlined the fact that he didn't need to be assured that I loved him, and maybe didn't need my love at all.

"I love you" implies certainty to a feeling that is, at best, amorphous and intangible. Telling someone you love them reduces it to an insecure need to feel part of something that you can't explain.

I should feel comforted by the idea that the chemicals in my own brain are responding only to visual and audio input, convenient interpretations of information influenced by the history of my life, and pheromones, all of which manipulate the chemicals in my brain to react in certain ways to incite certain feelings that my brain is already set up to feel.
I should be comforted, but I'm not.

What draws me to Mickey is his tendency to forgive me after I do something stupid or cruel.

But his tendency to forgive me after I do something reckless or immature is what drives me to do reckless and immature things, to see how much he'll take from me, to test the limits of my recklessness and immaturity.

When will it be too much? At what point will he leave me for good?

At what point will he recognize that my reckless and immature behavior is just a poorly designed cover-up for my many insecurities?

At what point will he say, "I know what you're doing and fucking stop," and lead me off into the sunset to live happily ever after?

I'm going to call my art show "MICKEY" and when Mickey notices that the work in the show has little to do with him and confronts me about it, I'll pretend I'm getting a phone call and the pretend phone call won't go well and I'll start crying loudly and ask Mickey if he'll drive me to the nearest bus stop and, I don't know, maybe I'll find purpose and meaning at the bus stop.

I dreamt I saw Mickey after several years of not seeing him. He had decided to become Hispanic for something having to do with fashion. He looked like a different person, but I hugged him and felt a strong, familiar sadness.

There was so much I wanted to say to him, but our conversation was minimal and strained because he kept slipping into Spanish, which I couldn't understand.

"You didn't used to be Hispanic," I said.

"Well," Mickey said, "You didn't used to be [indiscernible Spanish word[s]]."

While making breakfast tacos, I thought of how, when I had to sing a Pocahontas song in the fifth grade in front of the whole school, I pretended not to know some of the lyrics after a last-minute decision that that was the cool thing to do. I was simultaneously calculating how much spinach I would need for three breakfast tacos and whether or not I should cut open my avocado. An avocado grown from the earth which I now possessed legal ownership over, probably. Although, maybe you need paperwork to make something legal.

All of this was evidence that I had many, many important and interesting things to think about instead of Mickey.

I considered texting Alexei. I thought there was probably a forty percent chance he had not noticed my eight-month absence at all.

Or maybe I would wait even longer, see how long I could stretch the gap before contacting him became impossible because he moved away, or changed his phone number, or he started seeing someone who wouldn't allow him to talk to me, or I forgot about him.

"You could say that my relationship with him was contained in this gap in communication, that I treasured our gap and nurtured it as well as I could, learning new things all the time about how best to care for it," I would say in interviews about art I made about the gap, interviews that took place long after I stopped nurturing the gap or whatever the hell I was talking about.

The recipe for yogurt calls for yogurt.

Which seems like a metaphor for all the most horrifying universal truths.

And calls into question the very nature of being.

Like, without already having a small amount of what you envision your ideal self to be, you can never be it.

Or, you can't experience love unless you've already experienced love.

Ultimately, we are each just so horrifically alone. No one else can ever understand. You have only yourself to answer to, and only yourself to love and respect.

And if you are seeking external validation then you are not reading the yogurt recipe correctly.

I have a memory of being a kid, maybe nine or ten, and trying to get my mom to swim with me in the ocean. We were in Santa Cruz for the weekend with my mom's boyfriend, Lance, and his son, Brian. My mom kept telling me to play with Brian, who was four and who I hated for various reasons.

"I'll be out in a minute," she said.

"No, right now," I yelled from the water.

I've always remembered that day with embarrassment. I shouldn't have been so desperate and needy. I should have let my mom enjoy her vacation. I should have made friends on the beach, as other more well-adjusted children might have done.

More recently, I've remembered it with guilt. Maybe that day was representative of my regular behavior. Maybe I pushed my mom too hard to be someone she didn't want to be. Maybe she hated swimming in the ocean and I was too self-centered to have ever asked.

Even more recently I've remembered it with irritation. Why had she bothered taking me to the ocean? Was I meant to be Brian's babysitter on my mom and Lance's romantic vacation?

More recently still, I focused on a single detail of the memory, this particular facial expression my mom made in Lance's direction as I tried to physically pull my mom to the ocean. I could not interpret the expression at the time, and my memory of it now is too diluted by years of emotions to be reliable.

I wonder if I should include estranged relatives on my list of exes.

Untitled #17

I'M SORRY ABOUT THESE ARTWORKS, I HAD A FLAWED
PERSPECTIVE WHEN I MADE THEM.

Untitled #18

PLEASE REST ASSURED THE ARTIST IS ASHAMED OF WHAT
SHE HAS CREATED.

I texted my cousin Janine and asked her to forward my mom's phone number to me. I didn't explain why I didn't have it, or include any kind of pleasantry. I was embarrassed by my situation and embarrassed of the desperation I might have been revealing to my cousin.

As I waited for a response, I entertained some mean and juvenile thoughts about Janine and decided that I would never initiate contact with Janine again.

Janine sent the number and asked me how I was doing. I wrote down the number on a piece of paper in case my phone died or I smashed it against something in an unpredictable fit of emotion. I didn't answer Janine's text.

I listened to the Matchbox 20 song "If You're Gone," analyzing the lyrics as if they were my mom's secret message to me that she had been waiting for me to hear, or her secret message to herself if she ever listened to the song to try to gain perspective in life, or my secret message to her, because why not, it's not as if any of this made sense.

> I think you're so mean
> I think we should try
> I think I could need this in my life
> And I think I'm scared
> Do I talk too much?

I pressed her numbers into my phone and stared at them. I pushed the Send button while looking at something on the other side of the room, as if my physical actions were acci-

dental and totally beyond my control, and I was just dealing
with the phone call the universe had unfairly handed to me.

"Hello?"

"Hi. Mom?"

There was a silence that lasted, realistically, probably twelve seconds, but it felt more like three minutes in the moment, and during that time I maintained three inner monologues:

1. A pep talk about how I shouldn't be afraid to be a bitch.
2. Preparation for an argument with Courtney about how sometimes it feels like she views me as a projection of all her own worst qualities.
3. A layered soundtrack of my own nervous laughter from over the years.

"Oh. Hi."

"What are you doing?"

"Um. I just came home from the grocery store. I'm about to make spaghetti with turkey meatballs and Parmesan chips."

My inner monologue started giving another pep talk about how it was also okay to not be a bitch if I didn't feel like it.

My heart began beating so loudly I could hear it in the phone. I was afraid my roommates might hear it too, so I held my free hand to my chest to try to settle my heart.

"What are Parmesan chips?" I said.

"They're just piles of Parmesan cheese baked in the oven until they get a little crispy."

"Oh, cool."

"Yeah."

"Do you add something to the cheese to make it crispy?"

"No, and you don't need oil, either. It's just cheese."

"I should try to make that sometime."

"It's really easy," she said.

It wasn't the conversation I wanted to be having, but I couldn't stop myself from keeping it going. It felt like its own force. Where could we go from here? What else in the world did we possibly have to talk about?

"What temperature do you set the oven at?" I said.

"I preheat it to about 375 and bake for like, five minutes."

"Wow, sounds easy," I said. "Almost too good to be true."
I think we were still talking about cheese.

"Hey, I have to go, I'm getting another call," my mom said. Apparently it wasn't the conversation about cheese she wanted to be having.

Or it was the conversation about cheese she wanted to be having, but I wasn't the person she wanted to be having it with.

Either way, I blamed her (with the help of the portion of my inner monologue that wanted me to be a bitch) for everything that was wrong with my personality, everything that had ever gone wrong in my life, and everything that still had the chance to go wrong in the future.

"Okay," I said. "Bye."

"Bye."

Untitled #19

IT HAS TAKEN EVERY OUNCE OF MY COURAGE AND
STRENGTH TO DRAW THIS MALLARD WEARING A BUCK-
ET HAT.

HAVE I DISAPPOINTED YOU?

IF I HAVEN'T, WHEN WILL YOU ADMIT THAT I HAVE?

AND WHEN WILL YOU SEE THAT YOUR PROBLEM WITH
THE MALLARD WEARING A BUCKET HAT STEMS FROM
SOMETHING VERY WRONG INSIDE OF YOU AND HAS
NOTHING TO DO WITH ME OR THE MALLARD IN THE
BUCKET HAT?

IF THIS IS ANNOYING TO YOU THEN YOU CAN LEAVE.
NO JUDGMENT.

I KNOW THIS ISN'T FOR EVERYONE.

Every year before Christmas my mom would take me to see snow. She's from the East Coast, and she thought it was an important part of the holiday season that she wouldn't allow me to miss out on. It never snowed where we lived and sometimes the closest snow was on the side of a mountain hundreds of miles away. It didn't matter. We always went.

"This is a snow cactus," she said on one of our earlier trips, sticking pieces of twig onto a tall pile of snow she created. It's my first memory of feeling inspired.

When I was eight we made snow shoulder pads and she taught me how to wear them like a "fancy lady." The next year we brought plastic squirt bottles filled with food coloring and painted in the snow.

When I was ten she told me it was my turn to decide what to build. I brought some of my old clothes and we filled them with snow and made a group of upright snow people in a line facing the lake.

"They're waiting in line at the food bank for their holiday baskets," I said.

"You're such an artist," my mom said.

When Mendeleev created the Periodic Table of Elements, spaces were left blank for elements awaiting discovery. Elements that just seemed like they should exist. It's a little unbearable to compare my own human deficiencies to the precise and undeniably mathematical Periodic Table of Elements, because it seems probable that there was some kind of scientific evidence that the undiscovered elements existed, or were likely to exist. But it's like there are empty spaces in my life that I am purposefully leaving open, thinking that if the space is kept available, something can or will eventually find its home there.

Maybe the benefit of being someone who has been forced to be alone so frequently is that she finally learns how to be alone.

Maybe I can't seem to exile Mickey from my thoughts because I am aware of how painful it is to be forgotten.

Maybe, deep down, in the most elusive, neglected, unimaginable recesses of my heart, I am not an ugly and worthless piece of shit, but a kind and sympathetic piece of shit.

A piece of shit worth knowing.

"I finally got in touch with my mom," I said.

"How did it go?" Courtney said.

"We talked about cheese," I said. I knew that Courtney would interpret my statement as a dramatic oversimplification meant to be funny, and that would cause her to not take our conversation seriously, which would frustrate me because suddenly the only thing that was clear to me was that I wanted her to take it seriously.

But I decided to let her believe that what I said wasn't the whole story because the fact that we only talked about cheese was too embarrassing and painful to admit.

At my art show, I want there to be a big sign next to the refreshments that looks identical to the art that says:

PLEASE TAKE AS MANY CRACKERS AND SQUARES OF CHEESE AND GLASSES OF WINE AS YOU WANT. THESE ARE HERE FOR YOU. THE ARTIST WOULD BE MISERABLE IF SHE KNEW THAT YOU WERE NOT TAKING AS MANY CHEESE SQUARES AS YOU WANTED. THINK OF THIS WHOLE SHOW AS A MEANS FOR THE ARTIST TO GET THE CHEESE TO YOU. THE ARTIST BELIEVES THIS IS HER CONTRIBUTION TO THE WORLD.

Untitled #20

WOW! THE *NEW YORK TIMES* CALLS THIS ROSEMARY CHIVE CRACKER A TOUR DE FORCE!